Georgie

A Gathering Storm
...in the sky...in the man!

Bradley Farm Series
Book 6

MARY JANE FORBES

Todd Book Publications

Georgie
A Gathering Storm
...in the sky...in the man!

This is a work of fiction. All of the characters, names, locations, incidents, organizations, and dialogue in this novel are either the products of the author's imagination or are used fictitiously. The views expressed in this work are solely those of the author.

ISBN: 978-0-9847948-8-1 (sc)
Printed in the United States of America
Todd Book Publications: 4/2017
Port Orange, Florida

Author photo: Geri Rogers
Cover design 2018 by Angie: pro_ebookcovers

Georgie

A Gathering Storm
...in the sky...in the man!

Chapter 1

———

THE SOIL'S AROMA, rich with decaying leaves, is perfume to a farmer's soul. Fiery red maple leaves still clinging to the trees dappled with brilliant orange of the setting sun, bright yellows of quaking aspens. Georgie sucked in the warm fall air, hands on his hips, smears of grease across his brow, hands, and khaki work pants.

Edgy, scowling, Georgie took no notice of fall's beauty. Unshaven, stubble on his chin, black hair yanked into a ponytail, he stood next to the tractor. It was a relic but he took pride in keeping her purring out in the fields of hops and barley for Bradley Farm's brewpub.

Tugging a small scrap of towel hanging out of his back pocket, he wiped his hands, turned setting out in long strides to the quintessential, century old farmhouse, the white clapboards gleaming in the sunshine. Gran promised him some chocolate chip cookies in the late morning, and he figured it was late enough. Maybe a bit of sweet chocolate on his tongue would tamper his sour mood.

Stomping the loose dirt from his boots at the back door, he followed the scent of cookies like a bloodhound tracking his prey. Nodding to the two women sitting across from each other at the kitchen's long harvest table, he helped himself to a mug of coffee on the counter.

"Did you get her running?" Gran asked, grinning as she slid the plate of cookies toward him. She wasn't his grandmother, but everyone, relative or friend, called the matriarch of the family Gran.

"Like a cat purring by the fireplace," Georgie said.

"I still think we should invest in a new tractor," Jane said, tapping a pencil on the pad of paper in front of her. Her clear blue eyes glanced at Georgie. Dropping the pencil, she anchored a wayward curl of red hair sprinkled with strands of gray behind her ear. "With all the work you do, you deserve better equipment."

Gran, now a young eighty-something, sat across the table from her daughter-in-law, squaring her own pad of paper jotting down a note.

"Looks as if you two are planning—" Georgie started to say.

"Making our lists for Thanksgiving," Jane said leaning back, circling one of the entries.

Georgie shook his head, held his tongue from a sharp remark. He loved the two women who helped raise him. Today he thought them silly, decked out in their flowery kitchen aprons tied back with a bow, cookie dough smeared on their bibs. When they baked cookies it was always a few dozen—treats for the large Bradley Farm family. He knew he was lucky to be considered one of them. But today he didn't care, well, maybe he cared a little.

"The pies. What about something different this year, Gran?" Jane asked.

"Rhubarb pie? You like rhubarb pie don't you, Georgie? Of course, we'll still bake pumpkin, mincemeat, apple...*and* rhubarb," Gran said raising her brow.

Georgie shrugged his shoulders. It irked him to be called Georgie like he was still a kid. He was forty-six. It was time he brought it to their attention. Ask them to call him George.

"Maybe not fresh rhubarb. Jane and I cooked up several batches last year—stored the jars in the root cellar."

"Georgie, would you go down, bring up a couple of quarts?" Jane said. "I'll make a pie for dinner tonight. See if Danny likes it."

Georgie smirked. "Jane, that husband of yours likes everything you fix. I've never known him to complain," he said with a sharp tongue, grabbing another cookie as he headed to the back door.

Gran and Jane looked at each other, foreheads furrowed. Something was bothering Georgie these days, but they didn't know what.

Georgie never took the cellar stairs from the kitchen—too rickety and dark. He preferred to pull up the bulkhead hatch around the side of the house. Lifting the bulkhead allowed the cellar to fill with light.

Stepping down the creaky boards into the musty cellar, he looked to his left, to the shelving built by the first Bradley. Marshall Bradley bought the land and built the house. The shelves were constructed from rough hewn planks anchored to sections of trees, most of the bark still clinging to the trunks.

Georgie froze.

A large section of shelving, weakened by years of wood rot, had collapsed under the weight of crates of potatoes, squash, and an assortment of other root vegetables. The shelves holding some of the jars of preserves alongside the quarts of rhubarb had fallen down with the crates. Many of the jars had broken leaving the odor of rotting, sticky sweet fruit. But Georgie's eyes were not riveted on the mess of potatoes scattered across the dirt floor or the broken jars laying in front of him.

A small section of boards nailed together had been torn away from the trunks, torn away with the force of the collapsing planks exposing a gaping hole behind the debris. No one had ever seen the door built of shiplap, at least Georgie had never heard Gran or Jane speak of it. The shelves were built, as far as anyone knew, to hold the crates of food stored in the root cellar for the long New England winters.

Georgie looked to the bulkhead steps for the battery-powered lantern. It came in handy when more light was needed to see in the corners of the cellar. Danny, Jane's husband, affectionately known as Pops to the Bradley clan, had hung the lantern when his wife complained she couldn't see the labels on the jars. Holding the lantern, Georgie shoved the empty crates aside, as well as the planks of shelving. Setting the lantern on the floor, he pushed aside a few tree trunks crisscrossed as if they had been felled in a bad winter storm.

Now he could shine the light in the hole, large enough to walk through if he bent his head. The hole didn't open to a tunnel, more like a narrow room about three feet wide. Georgie picked up the lantern, ducking his head as he stepped into the hollow. He figured the space to be seven feet long. If he stretched out on the dirt floor, his six-foot-one frame would leave several inches to spare.

A rusty tin at the far end, the size of a shoe box, caught the lantern's light. Setting the lantern on the floor, he knelt down, tried to pry open the box. The lid wouldn't give. Glancing around for something to jam under the lip, there was nothing he could see that would do the trick. Undoing his belt, he jammed the edge of the buckle under the front of the lid, working it around until it popped up.

The tin contained several pieces of yellowed paper. Picking up the top sheet, he carefully unfolded it, his fingers gently smoothing the creases, revealing a drawing, a map. The other pieces looked to be identical. The map had several circles, one labeled *Bradley Station*. At the top of the map was written— Underground Railroad to Canada.

Chapter 2

THE YELLOWED PIECES OF paper were folded in half and half again, a size that could be stuffed in a coat or pants pocket. Georgie eased down onto the dirt floor sitting cross legged. Leaning against the dirt wall, he cradled the tin box on his lap and examined the map. There was a squiggly line on the left. A river? A few lines fanned out to the right. On each line was a large circle, one identified as *Bradley Station*.

Georgie leaned his head back against the cool, damp, dirt wall. *Underground Railroad*. He had heard the term and equated it to black people fleeing from the south to the north, to perceived freedom from the slave owners. Was Bradley Farm one of the safe houses? A safe place to hide in this dug out hollow? Not a tunnel because there was no exit.

"What happened here?" Georgie mumbled. He looked around the small cavern brightly lit with the LED lantern casting shadows out the hole into the cellar—small trees and pine shelves piled grotesquely one over the other. "Did people really hide in here, maybe a candle for light? Running away leaving everything behind? They must have been scared, terrified, huddled together. Kinda like Dad and me. Him wandering down the road, carrying me as a newborn in a basket, nothing but the shirt on his back, or so Gran told me."

The thought of the similarity made his heart race—sitting on the dirt, knowing others sat on this very spot. He could almost feel their breath on his cheek.

"Hey, Georgie, are you down there?" It was Finn, Jane and Danny's youngest son. At forty-one, he had renovated a barn down by the road into a brewpub. It became Georgie's job to supply the hops and barley grain to the brewery operation. A purpose he loved, farming the land, tilling the soil.

"Yep," Georgie called out. "Get Danny. You gotta come down. See what I uncovered."

"Pops is here. So are Mom and Gran."

"Bring 'em all. Careful, there's glass and boards all over the floor, and don't slip on the rhubarb," Georgie yelled.

Georgie stared at the opening listening to the commotion on the other side as Finn moved planks out of the way clearing a wider path for them.

"What the—" was all Finn could say. Behind him the other three crowded at the opening, gawking around his shoulder, heads bent straining to see.

A cave carved out of the ground?

"What's that you're holding, Georgie?" Danny asked.

Georgie handed the yellowed sheet to him. Danny held it at arm's length so they could all see, their heads tight together.

"Bradley Station?" Jane said.

"Look, Underground Railroad Map to Canada at the top," Gran said, leaning in against Jane with Finn's arm around her so she didn't fall.

Pops looked up over his glasses at Georgie. "A real map? Of what, exactly?"

"The big circle is labeled Bradley Station, I think. Hard to make out the script," Gran said.

"What else is in the box?" Finn asked.

Georgie lifted five more yellowed sheets, each folded as the first—in half, and half again. He handed one to Finn.

"This reminds me of the bones...the bones Arnie and I found, actually that Dog found...you remember Dog digging in the cellar,

Danny? You and Jane were dating. Just babies." Gran sighed with a chuckle. "You called the stray, Dog. We all did."

"Gran, I was eighteen," Jane said with a little elbow bump to Gran's arm. "Not a baby."

"And I was nineteen. Hardly a baby," Danny said, chuckling along with his wife.

Jane stepped back. "Looks like there won't be any rhubarb pie tonight, Gran."

"Georgie, how about you and I clean up this mess—" Finn began.

"Right-O. Then I'm going to do a little trolling on the internet…maybe go to the library," Georgie said.

"Ah, ask that nice librarian and her little boy to Thanksgiving dinner, if you have a mind," Gran said.

Georgie glanced at her, hesitating. "Ummm, I will… maybe," he said swiping dirt from his knees and backside.

Chapter 3

———

A STRONG WIND SWEPT through the barren branches stripping the few remaining leaves, tapping the windows of the little house, mere yards from the main farmhouse. It was not known which Bradley patriarch dubbed the small house as the tree house. But it was believed, from the time the property was purchased, to be where Marshall Bradley lived as he oversaw the building of the large farmhouse at the top of the hill.

More than once Gran told Georgie how he and his dad came to live and work on Bradley Farm forty-six years ago. Georgie's dad, known only as Wolfe, was offered the tree house as a place to live while he worked for the family. It was in rough shape, thought by the Bradley clan to be destined for the bulldozer. But Gran made Wolfe the offer that if he provided the labor, she would provide the materials to make the little house livable.

Wolfe accepted the offer feeling he'd found a home. Gran's husband had died a couple of months later, and her son, Danny, was away at war. Gran and Jane were desperate for help as debts mounted. They were in danger of losing the house and the farm.

Wolfe tackled the project, first providing a room to sleep for himself and his baby. In the years that followed, Georgie played and went to school with the Bradley children as they grew from babies to adults. Young Georgie helped his dad who continued to renovate the little house to include a bedroom for each, a living room, and a small galley kitchen. It was austere but comfortable for father and son. Wolfe counted his blessings.

Early on Georgie showed an affinity for the land. In his high school years, he began farming in earnest, providing produce for

Gran and Jane to sell in the small road-side stand, alongside the barn where Jane opened an antique shop. Initially Jane sold items stored in the attic of the large farmhouse, as well as those stashed in every nook and cranny of the barns that had been built over the years.

Wolfe kept up the repairs on the farm and kept up Danny's spirits when he returned from the war with the loss of a leg. The pair took to building reproductions when the antiques were gone. Gran told all of her grandchildren the story of how Wolfe and Georgie came to live on the farm.

Tonight, to the tapping of tree limbs against the window panes of his small bedroom, Georgie tossed and turned, dozing off now and then only to awaken with a start from a vivid dream of people running through the thick forest, frightened people.

At 2:16 a.m. Georgie swung his legs over the edge of the bed. Scrubbing his scalp under unwieldy, kinky-black hair, Georgie shot to his feet. He headed to the coffeemaker in a nook of his room, stopping to press the start button on his laptop. Sleeping lightly became a habit he developed while studying for school. He didn't want to wake his dad when he had the urge to study or use the internet for research so contained his nightly activities to his room.

Setting a mug of steamy coffee on the desk, he googled *Underground Railroad*. Many websites, articles, books popped up. Scrolling through the list, clicking on a few entries, reading the text displayed, only served to whet his appetite for more. He learned that in 1787, New Hampshire, as well as several other northern states, voted to abolish slavery. These new free states became safe havens for fleeing slaves. They were free by law if they made it to the north. It was a *big if*.

Many did make it, thanks to the Underground Railroad, but they had to hide from bounty hunters who were paid handsome sums if they found and returned the slaves to their owners.

After several hours, eyes smarting from staring at the monitor, Georgie decided to pursue his research elsewhere—the Lakeville librarian, and the professor he had befriended while taking courses at the University of New Hampshire studying for a four-year bachelor degree. The framed degree wasn't important to him. He did it for his dad. What was important was learning the latest methods, techniques of farming. Now that Finn had opened a brewpub, his needs for hops and barley increased each season, plus his partner and brewmaster, Cameron Foster, kept asking for different strains of seeds to create various flavors of specialty craft beers.

With the library at the top of the list, Georgie decided to stop by today. Besides the research, this would give him the opportunity to ask Emma, the librarian, if she'd like to come to the farm, along with her young boy, for Thanksgiving dinner with the Bradleys.

Another item on the list was to decipher the map in the tin box. He had an inkling that the small circle, near the big circle labeled Bradley Station, might be the tree house. Maybe the crawl space under the house was another hiding place. As a kid, he ventured into the hollowed out space, but never stayed long—too creepy. But now there was a reason to check it out. Maybe he'd find more clues, if indeed it served as a hiding place on the Underground Railroad.

Shutting down his computer, Georgie turned off the light and went back to bed. There were two hours before he had to get up. But sleep was fitful as images and words he had stumbled on in his research fought for dominance in his brain.

Chapter 4

A SMILE SPREAD ACROSS Georgie's face as he turned his previously owned black Ford pickup onto a strip of cement, the parking lot for the Lakeville Library. The fitful sleep, the frightened faces of women and children running for their lives in the forest were left behind with his second cup of morning coffee.

He liked the idea of asking Emma and her young boy to Bradley Farm for Thanksgiving. He knew a few things about her. She was a widow, a librarian, a devoted mother, and a pretty woman with light brown hair that grazed her shoulders. He had met her for coffee a couple of times, mostly to discuss the books she had on agriculture. The thought made him laugh. Not exactly romantic dates, if you could even call their discussions a date. Turning forty-six had given him pause. Pause, wondering if he was ever going to meet someone he'd feel strong enough about to ask her to marry him. Shuddering at the thought of marriage, his mind wandered to the girls in high school, then jumped to three young women he'd dated when he was attending the community college.

He'd sowed some wild oats those two years. Didn't find love but learned a lot about sex. The girls loved his perceived carefree personality, his ready wit. They fell for the dark handsome young man. Falling hard enough to entice him into their arms and maybe a wedding bed? But Georgie was careful sowing his oats. He saw his place on Bradley Farm tilling the soil and he didn't want to mess that up. Fatherhood would come when he was ready. In the meantime he had played the field, literally.

He assumed the role of big brother to Finn. The two never spent a day together that they didn't collapse in fits of laughter. But when Finn's dream of a brewpub came to fruition, Georgie's plans for the future crystallized as well. His love for the land now became a vocation and he signed up for classes at the University of New Hampshire. He couldn't play around just tilling the soil, he had to learn about crop rotation, how many plantings a year he could harvest, what he could do during the winter months to prepare for the next season. Professor Nancy Tainter was eager to help.

He learned that a farmer lived and breathed the weather. Of course, there was the lighter side every fall—the pumpkin patch. Families came every year with their kids to pick out the perfect pumpkin.

With a sigh, he pushed Nancy from his mind and entered the library, his garage-sale brown fedora in hand. Emma, pretty as a picture in a powder-blue wool dress, stood on a short stepladder between two bookshelves, the ever present cart of returned books alongside. She looked up at the sound of the door's buzzer, smiled as she stepped down to greet Georgie.

A twinkle in his eye, he strode to her, greeting her with a quick hug.

"You have mischief in your black eyes, Georgie," she said laughing. "What's on your mind?"

"A couple of things, Ms. Emma. I have something to show you." Georgie strode to an old-as-time golden oak table. He laid his hat down and pulled out a yellowed piece of paper from a manila folder. "Take a look at this and tell me what you see."

Emma took the piece of paper, sat down at the table, carefully smoothing out the creases. "Where did you get this, Georgie? It's very old."

"In the cellar of the farmhouse—a hidden room behind some shelving. I wondered if you have any books on the Underground Railroad. Also, do you have access to newspaper articles around 1840?"

Emma leaned back in the chair. "This big circle, Bradley Station. Are you thinking the farm could have been a safe house for runaway slaves?"

"That's what I'm thinking. So, do you…"

"No, not what you're looking for. There is a novel about plantation slaves making their way to the northern states and Canada, but I don't have access to newspapers that far back. Your best chance for information would be in Portsmouth—the library, or stopping at the Portsmouth Herald. They might have something in their archives."

"I thought about that, but I wanted to stop here first."

"You said you had a couple of things—what else can I do for you?"

"The Bradleys wanted me to ask you and your son to Thanksgiving dinner. I don't know the time—"

"Oh, I can't. I promised my in-laws I'd bring their grandson with me to spend Thanksgiving with them. Can I take a rain check, not for Thanksgiving, but for dinner another time?"

"Sure thing. Nice you have a family—important for your boy to remain connected to his grandparents."

"Yes, it is," Emma said. "They love him—hugs, kisses, and treats. They definitely spoil him. I love that he has the connection to his father's side. My husband was in the service, Pease Air Force Base. When he died, it was all I could to do to get out of bed in the morning. I was working part time at the library here. The librarian left and I took her place. The years slipped by…"

"Where are your parents, If you don't mind my asking?"

"I don't mind. They live in Vermont, not too far away, so my son spends weekends with them from time to time. My grandparents live close to them, too."

"Your son is a lucky little fella." Georgie turned away, noting the warmth in her eyes and more. He wasn't ready for more.

"I'll be back in touch. Let you know what I find in Portsmouth. Now, can I checkout that novel?"

Georgie left with the book in his hand, his hat on his head, and a knot in his stomach. He looked up at the skiffs of puffy white clouds skittering across the sky. Another beautiful fall day. A whisper of cold air tickled his ears. He hunched his shoulders against the chill. Winter was coming. Sliding onto the truck seat, he frowned as he inserted the key, the truck springing to life. *Nice,* he thought, imagining the grandparents wrapping their arms around their twelve-year-old grandson. *The grandparents would be about Gran's age. Maybe I have a grandmother...somewhere.*

Pressing the gas pedal, he backed out of the parking spot, turned onto the two-lane road to the farm.

Chapter 5

BACK AT THE FARM, Georgie headed down to the horse barn, the barn Wolfe had set up as a woodworking shop for Danny when he was recuperating from his wounds in the war, rehabilitation using the prosthesis attached to his stump. Recuperating mentally as much as physically, or so Gran's story went when Georgie was old enough to understand.

In the shop Georgie found his dad and Danny, their feet up on stools, sharing a discussion on wood finishes—stain and wax, or stain and polyurethane. They stopped when Georgie ambled in.

"Anything you want me to do before I go on a scavenger hunt?" Georgie asked with a grin.

Danny chuckled. "That map's got you thinking hasn't it? Anything of interest at the library, like a certain librarian?"

"Emma gave me a couple of ideas of where to look for information and a book on the Underground Railroad she had on the shelves."

"And what about Thanksgiving?" Wolfe slid in the question, his voice soft. His voice was always soft. A person had to pay attention or they'd miss something he said.

"Gave her a rain check on dinner. She's spending the day with her late husband's parents. They wanted to spend some time with their grandson. So, if you two will excuse me, I have a map burning a hole in my pocket."

"Give a yell if you find anything—trap door, another map, hopefully not another pile of bones," Danny said, chuckling again.

"Maybe you'd better stop by Finn's house, pick up Lucas. That little fella has a helluva nose," Wolfe said.

———

GEORGIE LEANED ON THE trunk of a large old maple tree, map in hand, eyes staring at the back of the tree house, the only home he'd ever known. Lucas sat next to his boot, tail swishing the fallen leaves, waiting for the game to continue.

The map had a line from the big circle meandering northeast to the edge of the paper. There were two big circles from the lower left corner of the paper to the Bradley Station label. The lines continued on to the upper right hand side with two more large circles. The other circles were not marked. There was no line from Bradley Station to the small circle which almost touched the big circle on the map. Did that indicate a safe place near the big house? Was it the tree house? It had to be.

The front door of the tree house faced up the hill, sight line to the farmhouse. If someone was hiding and had to make a run for it, he surely wouldn't leave by the front door. He'd be seen.

Georgie slowly stepped to the back of the house, around each side, scrutinizing every foot for a trap door in the ground, or something near the crawl space under the house. The house was small—two bedrooms, a living room, bathroom and kitchen. Not much bigger than Finn's tiny house. There was an attic, but Wolfe left it alone when he made the house habitable. Georgie and Finn had climbed the rickety stairs a couple of times, but it was too creepy for the youngsters, and they always made a hasty retreat back down the stairs, careful not to stumble. In their teenage years, and now as men, they'd forgotten about the creepy attic.

Wolfe, with Jane's help, had taken the pieces of furniture from the attic of the tree house down to the barn beside the road, now Jane's antique shop.

Georgie went inside his home, examining the walls in every room. Wolfe had stuffed insulation between the bare studding and then covered the walls with cheap wallboard panels popular years ago. Georgie knocked on all the walls. They were solid. The only place left to look was the crawl space accessible from the back. The house was leveled by building it on cement blocks taking into account the ground sloping down to the lake on the north edge of Bradley Farm.

Changing into the tattered khakis he wore when working on the tractor, Georgie went back outside, again walking around for a spot to crawl under. Lucas scampered through the leaves always returning to see where the human was going next.

Georgie tried to pull a bush back but it was prickly. Spotting some vines that had dropped its leaves, he wedged around them and on his belly managed to scrunch under the back left side of the house. Lucas mimicked his actions, following on his little furry belly.

There was more head room than Georgie first thought. Rolling on his side, propped up on his elbow, he fished his flashlight from his jacket and methodically beamed the light a foot at a time on the joists of the floor above his head. Nothing resembled a trapdoor. Scanning the beams again, slower this time, mumbling. "Lucas, that's Dad's bedroom, then the pipes for the bathroom and the kitchen sink to the septic tank, and the pipes for water pumped to the house from a well."

He inched forward a few feet more and then he saw it. About a four-by three-foot section of the floor was framed in a rectangle. If he was thinking straight, his bed sat over the rectangle.

George backed out of the crawl space, Lucas squirreling out ahead of him. Georgie brushed off his khakis with a couple of swipes, jogged to the front door and to his bedroom. Pulling his twin-size bed away from the wall, his eyes popped open.

"Yes, sir, Lucas. If I'm not mistaken this is a beautiful trap door. It could also be a repair for broken floorboards." Pulling his bed to the center of the room, he stared at what he thought was a door. How was he going to pry up the boards? "A crowbar might do it, Lucas."

Reaching for his cell on the dresser, Georgie called Finn for help, then called the horse barn for Wolfe and Danny. The men quickly gathered each with a crowbar in hand and one for Georgie. They discussed different ways to raise the heavy oak planking as Lucas yelped weaving between the men's legs. They decided to assume it was a door, so instead of breaking it apart with crowbars, they'd attach handles, keeping the crowbars as plan B. Wolfe had several old metal handles in his crate of hardware he'd assembled over the years. A treasure trove of rusty nuts and bolts, and handles to sift through when an odd piece was needed.

With handles attached, one on each end and two on the same side, the four positioned themselves beside the handles. The first try didn't work. They had to apply more muscle. Grunting, they managed to dislodge it a smidge, dropping it back down.

"It's definitely meant to be a trap door," Danny said. "Not sure we have the manpower to lift the sucker."

"Speak for yourself, Pops. I say on the count of three we give it another try—shoulder to the wheel, but DON'T let go, keep up the muscle power," Finn said.

"I'll count," Georgie said. "On the count of three we lift her, keep lifting until it's up on its side, keep on lifting until she's leaning against the wall. Got it?"

"Yea, yea," Finn said. "Start counting—"

"One. Two. Three!"

Straining, cussing, grimacing, the old door gave way. More cussing, grunting, they swung the door up on its side."

"Hold on," Danny said.

He and Wolfe on each end moved next to Finn and Georgie.

"Now, let's go! Ups-a-daisy," Danny said, his voice strangled.

With more guttural cursing and groaning—the four pushed the block of wood up against the wall.

Standing back, sucking in air, they looked down through the hole—plenty of room for a person to squeeze through. The men stood gaping at the dirt below—a hiding place, a place for a group to make a run into the thick forest more than a hundred years ago.

Chapter 6

———

FEEDING THE CHICKENS, checking the catalog from the seed supplier one last time, the rest of the chores could wait. Georgie was itching for more information on the Underground Railroad, especially how it might tie to Bradley Farm. He said goodbye to Gran and headed out to Portsmouth.

Parking in the central parking garage downtown, he set off at a fast pace to the Portsmouth library a few blocks away. Luckily, the librarian was available. He asked about the scope of information she had on the Underground Railroad, specifically information about runaway slaves from the South, the years 1840 to 1900. He was hoping for newspaper articles, and, if by any chance, full-page copies of the papers digitized with access on the internet. The librarian showed him around the stacks—novels, as well as books on New Hampshire's legal history for that period. She set him up at a computer station to research the vast information the library cataloged.

In searching the archives for articles on the Underground Railroad, he learned the *Portsmouth Herald* in 1884 was called the *Penny Post*. In another article, he saw that New Hampshire passed a law making it a safe state, meaning if runaway slaves crossed the border they were free. Full-page pictures in the mid-1880s were sketchy. Some of the articles broke his heart. Stories of abuse the slaves endured at the whip hands of some landowners. More horror stories describing their escapes, following maps as they fled from one station to the next, stations where they were fed, offered clean clothes, and then sent with new, updated maps to follow on their way north.

Rubbing his eyes, Georgie decided not to visit the Herald, at least not today. The library archives contained enough information for his purposes—the discovery of the life and times of the first Marshall Bradley. He now knew the extent of information the library offered and how to access it. He took out a library card and thanked the librarian.

It was after one o'clock when he left the library and he was starving. His head filled with the stories he'd read, he strolled to the parking garage but decided to stop at a coffee shop on Market Street he had visited before. His thoughts returned to his duties on the farm. He still had to till the soil adjacent to the barley acres and seed a cover crop before a hard freeze. Calling his professor on his cell as he walked, he made an appointment for next week to discuss the best cover crop to feed the soil over the long winter months. The real reason he wanted to meet with her was to ask her to Thanksgiving dinner. Professor Nancy Tainter was attractive, outgoing, and they had enjoyed many conversations over lunch. Gran was on his case, so he was going to surprise her at the dinner table tomorrow, telling everyone he'd invited a woman to Thanksgiving dinner.

Smiling at the thought, he picked up a newspaper inside the front door of the coffee shop to check the weather. The lunch crowd seemed to be lingering—no empty stools at the counter and all the tables were taken. Turning to his right, he saw a woman, a pretty woman, sitting alone at a table for four. She was gazing out the window a coffee mug in her hand. He sauntered over to the table, pulled out the chair opposite her.

"Excuse me," he said, his lips drawing up into a smile.

She looked up, brows raised.

"Would it be okay if I sat at the table—read my newspaper with a cup of coffee?"

She nodded, moved her purse off the table to the empty chair between them, and looked back out the window.

The waitress took his order for a black coffee and a bagel with cream cheese and chives. He opened the paper to the day's local news and weather.

Without moving her gaze from the window, the woman said, "Are you from Portsmouth?"

Georgie blinked. He drew a blank.

When he hesitated, she turned, looked at him. Again raising her brows. Did he hear her? It was a simple question.

"Well, ah, yes, sort of. Are you from here?" he asked. A polite question.

"For now. Does your family live here?"

He stumbled again, but nodded.

She turned back to the window, and Georgie turned to the weather forecast.

The waitress returned with his order, poured his coffee. She looked at the woman staring out the window again. "Rosie, would you like more coffee?"

The woman shook her head.

The waitress looked at Georgie. He nodded. She topped off his mug and moved on.

"Does your family live here?" Georgie asked. There was something about the woman, not so much a sadness as a blank— her face, her eyes.

"I have no family," she said.

He took a bite of his bagel.

Rosie continued to gaze out the window, then glanced sideways at him.

"What do you do, if you don't mind my asking?" she said.

"I don't mind. I'm a farmer."

"Portsmouth?"

"No, a small town west of here, Lakeville. Ever hear of it?"

She nodded.

"Do you work in town?" Georgie asked. The woman was beautiful, mysterious. The thought crossed his mind, if she smiled, if her eyes warmed a bit, any man would be caught in her spell. A beautiful face framed in soft waves of satiny black hair falling around her shoulders.

"I'm a nurse...for now."

"That's a wonderful profession. Here in Portsmouth?"

"Yes. I have to go." Rosie leaned over, picked up her purse, stood staring at him.

"It was nice to meet you, Rosie. My name is George," he whispered. He thought if he didn't whisper he'd scare her off.

"Yes, it was nice to meet you, George."

"Maybe we'll meet here again sometime?" he said.

"If you're around...Wednesdays...one-ish."

She looked at him, a slight smile, a friendly smile, eyes crinkled in the corners.

Yeah, a guy could fall for her. He watched her walk to the door. Such poise, style. Her black slacks flared at the ankle, the white cable knit sweater skimmed her thighs. She flipped the black and white plaid cape around her shoulders as she reached for the door handle pushing the door open.

When Rosie left the coffee house, the cozy atmosphere seemed to lose its warmth. Georgie raised his chin, inhaling the last of her scent. It's genesis elusive.

He suddenly felt alone in the hubbub, the chatter, the laughter filling the coffee house. Wednesday. One o'clock. He would be here.

Family? Rosie asked if he lived here. Wolfe was his dad. He considered the Bradleys his family, but that's because they considered his dad, and by extension himself, as part of the clan.

And that was because his dad happened to walk up the driveway one day. Yes, the Bradleys thought of them as family. But they really weren't. Did he have a family? Siblings? A Gran? Somewhere?

———

THAT NIGHT HE SAT at his computer, but only stared at the screen, the instructions to login to his account at the Portsmouth library lying next to his keyboard. So much information swirling in his head but he kept returning to the woman at the coffee shop he sat next to staring out the window. Rosie. Sighing, he shut down his computer and went to bed.

Several hours later his eyes popped open, heart pounding. Visions of faceless black people running, driven by fear, leaving everyone they knew behind.

"What am I running from?" he slurred.

Disoriented, still running in the dark, he slowly realized he was in bed. He lay in the dark until his heart returned to normal. Fishing his legs out from under the covers, over the edge of the bed, he planted his feet on the bare wood floor, dangling his hands between his legs, head bent.

How did he get in this state of confusion—depressed over everything. By nature, he was a glass-half-full kind of guy. When did that end?

He lay back in bed, hands behind his head.

He couldn't put his finger on it, but the empty feeling had begun building months ago. Was it after Finn married Katie, or when Sadie married Travis? Their lives were moving on, but his was not. He was on the outside looking in. But it was more than that.

He thought of Rosie—lost. That's what he felt—lost and alone. The feeling was dragging him down. He loved farming but it wasn't his farm—nothing was his. Emma, even Rosie, asked him about his family. Finn called him bro, but he wasn't a brother. He had his dad. But he was always distant, almost like Georgie didn't exist. He watched the Bradleys—always a hug, a touch, a kiss. He had none of that nor did he give any of that. There was a time that he and Finn were close—but was it family close or friend close? Was there a difference? One thing he knew—he didn't like the dark place he was in. He'd tried to kick it, but at the moment he didn't care.

Chapter 7

———

DR. NANCY TAINTER, his professor for crop management, was rumored to be a spinster—never married, no children. Georgie's friendship with her grew from the first day of the first class he attended in the bachelor degree program. Being twenty years older than her normal group of students, he stood out and easily caught her eye—a man in charge of farming crops for a brewpub on a family farm.

Meeting in her office on campus, visiting or matriculating, Georgie always felt connected, like he belonged to something bigger than himself. Having a friendly relationship with a professor made him feel special. Their conversations were always animated, each becoming excited discussing new methods of farming. New technology was bursting on the scene monthly, sometimes weekly on propagation of seedlings, how to nurture them to an outstanding crop. Methods of harvesting, storing, selling to customers in other states when there was an abundance, more than the brewpub could use, stirred their conversations.

He always left the professor with a feeling of renewal. There had been moments when he caught her looking at him, not as a student, but as a man. When this happened, he suddenly felt a similar attraction, looking at her as an attractive woman, but he never acted on the impulse. He'd wondered several times driving back to the farm why he didn't wrap her in his arms, kiss her thin lip line, making them flush, wanting more.

In mid-July, she had called about a study she found on new and improved supports to grow hops—rows on trellises. She greeted him with excitement, a hug, grasping his hand, leading him to the couch to examine the report lying on the coffee table. He had a sudden stab of desire. He grabbed the report, began pacing over the Oriental rug in the large office as he read. Under control quickly, he sat in a chair facing the couch. They discussed the report for almost an hour. When he left, he had hugged her briefly. At that moment, why didn't he step back into her office? She had moved close, their bodies almost touching, obviously willing, wanting to receive his kiss.

He shook his head. That was then. Now approaching the campus, her building, he mumbled to himself as he parked. "What's the matter with you, George Wolfe? Nancy is an interesting woman. You have the same likes. What's holding you back? You and she would make a great pair. I'll tell you why you're holding back. I don't look at her the way Danny looks at Jane, or Finn at his new wife Katie. Just say it. You don't look at Nancy like you did at Rosie yesterday. You wanted to know more about Rosie, even felt a need to shield her from what was bothering her. Oh, man. You're really getting ahead of yourself, old man."

Georgie knocked on the professor's heavy oak office door and went in.

She looked different today. There were no classes—a school holiday. In fact she had given the final exams. The students had their assignments—two reports due in January. Nancy was dressed casually, slacks, sweater conforming to her body. If she chose the sweater to get his attention, it worked.

The conversation was easy, both of them comfortable with the topic of a different cover crop to feed the soil over the long winter.

Nancy was the one to bring up the subject of Thanksgiving.

"Are you spending Thanksgiving with your family on the farm?" she asked, leaning back on the couch sipping a cup of coffee.

Georgie sat on a chair, the other side of the coffee table where he always sat.

"I'm glad you asked. You're probably going to Iowa, or wherever your family is these days, but if you don't have other plans, the Bradleys would like you to come to the farm for dinner."

"I'd love to, George. Farmers are known for their cooking, so I probably shouldn't bring pie, but how about a bottle of wine...or two?"

"That would be very thoughtful. I'm sure they would appreciate it."

"You're fortunate to work for such a lovely family as the Bradleys."

Georgie looked away. Work for a family? Why not my family?

"Did I say something wrong, George? You look, I don't know, like I hit a nerve of some kind."

Georgie gave her a wide smile. "Not in the least. It will be fun to show you around. I'll let you know the time. They'll be thrilled you're coming. I've talked about you and now they'll have a chance to meet you. I have something else to show you." Georgie pulled the map from his pants pocket, laid it on the table in front of her, smoothing the creases.

Nancy picked up the map. "Interesting. Where did it come from?"

"The cellar at the farmhouse, in a hidden room of sorts behind some collapsed shelving. I went to the library in town. Emma, the librarian loaned me a book on the Underground Railroad. I asked her to come to Thanksgiving dinner so I could show her where I found it."

"And, is Emma coming to dinner?"

"No, she's taking her young son to visit his grandparents. She's a widow."

"I see. So now you're asking me to Thanksgiving dinner. How charming. You know what, I forgot I was going to Harold's for Thanksgiving. He's a professor in the math department. Tenured. Sorry, George, I have to run, I have another appointment in town. See you in January."

———

DRIVING BACK TO THE FARM, a smile covered Georgie's face. He should feel stupid at mentioning Emma to Nancy, but in fact he was relieved. The minute Nancy said she'd love to come to dinner, he felt trapped. He couldn't think of a way to rescind the invitation, and never thought what he said about Emma could have ticked her off. Was she jealous?

Yes, he was relieved she wasn't coming, but he still felt like a jerk. *I'll stop at the brewpub, talk to Finn. He'd laugh, make me laugh, call me a guy meant to be a forever bachelor.*

But Georgie didn't want to be a bachelor. He thought of Rosie. She seemed lost. That's how he felt—lost.

Parking his truck by the farmhouse, he ambled down to the pub, sat at the bar. Finn came out from the back, smiled, then frowned. Georgie saw the frown, realized he was going to be peppered with questions. It was a mistake to think he could talk to Finn, share his feelings. He had to leave.

"What's the matter, bro?"

The question hit Georgie in the gut. If only he was Finn's brother. But he wasn't.

Chapter 8

A SHIVER RAN DOWN Georgie's back as he left the brewpub. He hated his gut reaction to Finn's friendly use of the word, bro. Pausing, hands on hips, he took a deep breath of the humid air. He looked to the sky. A few clouds, nothing to be alarmed about. His gaze turned to the fields of barley waving in the soft breeze. He planned on harvesting the bumper crop after Thanksgiving. If his timing was off it could mean a long winter, less funds for seeds in the spring. Worse, it could mean ruin. If waiting proved to be right, the next couple of weeks would unleash rapid growth to maturity. His target—providing funds for expansion. But did he dare chance it? The first year providing barley and hops to the brewery was crucial, giving Finn and Cameron the opportunity to grow their business.

Georgie sucked in a gulp of air, releasing it slowly—another shiver. The air was full of moisture. Cell in hand, he tapped the weather app. An early fall storm was building off the great lakes. Two systems were colliding, spawning heavy rain by morning. Tornadic activity coupled with hurricane force winds were likely.

Tapping the farm equipment rental number, he alerted Sam, a longtime friend, that he was on his way to pick up the harvesting equipment for the farm's barley crop. Sam said he saw the weather building but none of the other farmers had called.

"How long do you think you'll need the combine thresher?" Sam asked.

"My acreage isn't that big, not like some in the craft beer businesses growing their own barley. My last harvest took six hours. If I can pick up your combine within the hour, I figure, pushing it, I can finish in five. Sam, check her headlamps are working."

"Will do. I can send Henry over with a truck if you like. He's been asking when you planned to harvest. He could use a few extra bucks. It's slow here. Need anything else?"

"No, and Henry's help would be great. Your truck and mine will also speed up the process of getting the grain into the barn."

"Georgie, I'll drive the combine to the farm. Give you more time to organize the farmhands. I'll leave as soon as I talk to Henry, let him know the situation."

"Sam, you're a lifesaver."

Another tap on his cell, Georgie alerted his field manager they were harvesting immediately. "Larry, gather as many hands as you can get. We're harvesting the barley—starting in an hour. We'll keep working until we're done. There's a big storm heading our way. We're in danger of losing the whole crop if the predicted strength materializes—the field could be swamped. We can't take any chances on losing the whole damn crop."

"Georgie, you're a worry wart. It's pushing north—" Larry started to say.

"Larry, one hour. Round up the men. Warn them we'll work until we're done--tonight." Shoving his phone in his pocket, he strode back to the pub, yelling for Finn and Cameron as he entered.

Finn came around from the back of the bar. "What's up, bro?"

"Oh, just a damn tornado, maybe a hurricane—hell, it's big enough that I'm harvesting the barley, and stop calling me bro."

Finn's brows scrunched at the swear words, the snarky remark. "When?"

"Within the hour. Sam is sending Henry over with a truck—he's driving the combine and—"

"Hold on. Let me get Cameron." Finn tapped his phone. "Cam, can you come out front. Georgie's here. Says a storm—"

Finn looked at his phone. Cam had disconnected the call. He came bursting through the swinging door from the brewery.

"Georgie, it's too early. I just accepted an order for a load of barley—the guy's getting back to me with the number of bushels. He didn't want delivery this early. He stipulated—"

"If it storms, rains like hell, swamps the fields, there won't be any barley now, or a month from now. It'll rot." Georgie countered.

"You know we planned to expand the number of tanks to brew—" Cam started to say.

"I KNOW. And we were also planning to update the storage with refrigeration for the hops, and a temperature system for humidity control for the barley. It's a fairytale if we lose this crop, a bumper crop right now I might add, or the very real possibility of nothing." Georgie shouted.

Finn's eyes darted from Cam to Georgie. Finn turned to Cam, "Georgie's right. We can't take a chance on losing everything."

———

GEORGIE DROVE THE COMBINE hard, perched high in the machine's cockpit, threshing the barley, dumping as he went into grain carts hitched to the trucks. As soon as one cart was full, the truck took off to the barn dumping the load into the storage bins. Henry handled the other truck with a cart pulling into position to accept the next dump of barley from the threshed grain spewing out of the funnel. Sitting behind the wheel of the big combine, ears plugged against the grinding noise of the motor, Georgie navigated through the rows of barley, always keeping an eye to the west. A few dark clouds had moved in, the breeze gaining strength.

They were cutting it close.

A bolt of lightning, followed by claps of thunder, boomeranged in the distance.

The storm was picking up steam.

The sun disappeared behind billowing black clouds.

Dusk turned to night.

Georgie figured he had another hour before the field would be harvested, transported to storage before the rain came, and it was surely coming.

Periodically Jane hustled down from the house carrying thermoses of strong coffee. Gran, moving at a fast trot with the aid of her cane, met her half way down the path with cookies for the men. Both women hustling back to the house to brew more coffee.

"Another fifteen minutes, you bastard," Georgie called to the heavens. "Give me another fifteen minutes."

Lightning filled the coal-black sky. Not one bolt, but bolt after bolt. Sudden gusts of wind whipped over the field, each stronger than the last.

Georgie halted the big harvester. Jumping down he was hit in the face with a stinging downpour. He yelled at Henry driving the truck with a cart. "Get back to the barn. Hurry! Don't dump this load on top of the other. Unload it on the floor. It's wet. Then head back to Sam's shop," he hollered. "I'll return the harvester. Understand?"

"Yah, I got it." The truck spun its wheels as Henry stomped on the gas pedal.

———

ADRENALIN DEPLETED, GEORGIE bumped down the road to the equipment rental yard. Sam met him, opening the gate to the yard. Driving the combine through the gate, he shouted down at Sam alerting him that Henry should be back soon with the truck.

Sam nodded. "I'll take you back to the farm. Car's out front. Henry called. He's going straight home—bringing the truck back in the morning."

Sam dropped Georgie off at the end of the driveway of Bradley Farm. The rain was coming down in sheets, but Georgie insisted on walking. The rain felt good. He waved goodbye to Henry as he passed in the truck. Georgie strode up to the horse barn, his strides shorter, a little slower after the tension of the past hours. He turned on the lights, checked on the pile of barley on the barn floor from the last load. It wasn't as big as he thought. That meant he saved almost the entire crop. Satisfied, he shut off the lights and slid the barn door shut.

Turning down the path to the tree house, he saw the porch light was on. His dad always left the light on for him if he wasn't home before dark. It wasn't much, but it did show his dad cared— a little.

Chapter 9

A FULL BLOWN HURRICANE didn't develop, but the rain poured down nonstop for more than two hours. The family gathered around the breakfast table, mounting heaps of praise on Georgie for his quick action. Georgie seemed to be himself—not a man peppering his vocabulary with swearing. Of course, the pending storm had been a dire situation, a situation that would have ruined the plans for the bumper crop were it not for Georgie's quick action.

"Gran, I have a surprise for you. Don't go anywhere," Finn said. "Katie and I were out getting some groceries—before all the excitement with the storm. Don't move...promise?"

"My goodness, Finn. What have you been up to...I promise I won't move."

Finn dashed out, returning with a bundle of fluffy fur on a leash. The dog was the same size as Lucas but black instead of tan. Releasing the pup from the leash, he dashed around the table, in and out the chair legs, stopped, tail wagging. With a yelp he made a flying leap onto Gran's lap.

"Oh my...yes...nice doggie. What am I supposed to do with him, Finn? I can't—"

Finn and Georgie laughed as the pup licked Gran's face. "That does it. He's definitely your dog, Gran," Finn said.

"Well, he is rather cute. Where did you get him? Yes, yes, nice doggie."

"Beside the road. Just like Lucas. Katie spotted him—no tag. He looked a bit scruffy and definitely sad. Daisy gave him a bath last night, or let me say they gave each other a bath. She used bubble bath. Katie thought he'd make a nice doggie pal for Lucas. I thought you might like a furry friend, but Katie said to let the little guy choose. He's obviously chosen you, Gran."

"Well, you tell Daisy that I'll need her help taking care of him."

"What do you want to name him, Gran?" Jane asked.

"Oh, I don't know. He certainly seems to have a lot of energy the way he scoots around—that's it. I'll call him Scooter. Is Scooter okay with you, doggie?"

Scooter raised his head, licked Gran's cheek then settled on her lap, tongue hanging out.

"Poor thing is tuckered out. Must be the bubble bath," Danny said chuckling.

Georgie and Finn pushed back from the table, thanked Gran and Jane for the blueberry pancakes. Bussing their plates to the sink, they sauntered out the back door.

Lacing his fingers, stretching his arms out, Georgie looked at Finn. "You up for a scavenger hunt?"

"Always. What are we hunting for?" Finn replied a wide grin spreading across his face.

Georgie pulled the map from his pocket. "I don't know. Possibly a clue as to who hid in the tree house."

"Hmm, intriguing. You found a trapdoor. So you think more secrets are lurking in the shadows?" Finn said as he sent a text to his business partner, Cameron, tending the tanks in the brewery in back of the pub.

Cam, down in a few. Going with GW to tree house.

That done, Finn ran after Georgie already halfway down the hill without breaking his stride. "Hang on, bro. I'm coming," he said with a chuckle, hustling to catch up.

"I knocked on all the plastered walls Dad added when he renovated," Georgie said. "They seemed solid. Let's start our search with the crawl space. Once I saw the trapdoor under my bedroom, I stopped looking. We'll eyeball every square inch of the house, even the attic. I haven't been in the attic since we were kids."

"As I recall, Georgie, you were scared to go in the attic. Very creepy. Lots of cobwebs, spooky. Hey, where are you going?"

"Horse barn. We need a couple of flashlights."

Finn waited on the path. No point chasing after Georgie. When the guy was on a mission, his feet went into high gear.

Emerging from the horse barn, Georgie met up with Finn and continued at a fast clip to the back of the tree house.

Flashlights in hand, the pair shimmied into the crawl space on their backs. The trapdoor overhead, they crisscrossed their flashlights over the flooring above. Nothing obvious, they shimmied out swatting each other on the back to remove the dirt. Next stop, investigate inside the house.

Each took a room, their eyes wandering methodically over the walls, floors, ceiling, and around the windows. Other than the trapdoor Georgie had discovered, everything seemed solid, definitely newer than a hundred years ago, and no place to hide something. Georgie had questioned his father since finding the map about the renovations he did. Wolfe couldn't remember seeing anything unusual, amend that, everything was unusual with crawly critters, evidence of an invasion of squirrels, and agreed with Gran several times, that the place probably should have been bulldozed. But after his labors, the small structure was habitable, comfortable.

"Hey Finn, let's go up to the attic. Dad told me the last time he'd been in the attic was to help Jane remove the furniture. Danny said a couple of his friends came over to haul a dresser, some small pieces, and a bed down to Jane's antique shop.

Mounting the creaky stairs built against the living room wall, Finn reached out tickling Georgie's back.

"Hoo, hoo, said the owl." Finn chuckled, running his fingers up Georgie's arm. They laughed as Georgie pushed open the door at the top of the stairs.

The attic space was topped with the pitch of the roof, a small window centered on either side in the triangle formed by the pitch.

Wolfe told him he ran electricity to the attic, wired a light when the furniture was moved. Georgie reached for the string. The bare bulb came to life, illuminating a small area, casting shadows around the perimeter of the space.

"Just as we found it when we were kids," Finn said.

"It looks the same as when you and I ventured up here. Still creepy," Georgie said. "Some of the walls are covered with shiplap, some kind of plaster between the edges. You go to the left. I'll go to the right. We'll shuffle all the way around. It's a big enough space that several people could have hidden up here."

"Eerie to think of people hiding, sitting on the floor, maybe lying on a mat. Whoa!" Finn let out a squeal.

"What?" Georgie said looking sharply over his shoulder.

"A big square nail snagged my shirt. Ouch. Shine your light will ya? I can't hold the flashlight and pull my shirt—"

The thump of a picture hit the floor along with a piece of wood. Both men jumped.

"Finn, look here. Something's tucked in the space between the studs, behind that board that fell."

"Georgie, I'm bleeding where that big old nail scratched my tender skin," Finn said examining his tummy.

"Look, Finn." Georgie pulled out a small leather-bound book the size of a paperback.

Finn shined his flashlight on the book. Opening it, Georgie turned the first couple of pages, pages written in long hand with a pen.

"Finn, it's a journal. Here, read the first three lines."

Georgie turned the book so Finn could see. "July, 1841. My name is Rosemary Freedman. I was a slave but now I'm free."

Chapter 10

FINN GLANCED AROUND THE ATTIC. "Geez, Georgie, it's hard to believe what happened here. Good old great, great whoever was a real hero. I'll catch you later. I want to read that book—maybe there's more about Bradley Station. I have to get back to the brewery. We have another order for Cameron's new specialty beer—a pub in Wisconsin."

"Your partnering with Cameron and his wife Carrie, was sure a good move," Georgie said.

"You can say that again. That was some scavenger hunt, bro."

"Yep, it sure was. Thanks for coming with me," Georgie said.

"See you tonight at dinner. Bring the journal. It's going to blow the family away."

"Will do. Nice job with Scooter. You're such a softy," Georgie said, pulling the string leaving the attic in the shadows of the barren trees outside the windows. He followed Finn, clomping down the creepy attic stairs, then went to his bedroom and closed the door. He wanted to read the journal in private. Propping himself up on a couple of pillows, he opened the leather bound book.

———

July, 1841.

My name is Rosemary Freedman.

I was a slave but now I'm free.

Lewis was my surname, taken from the owner of the large plantation where I was a slave. Many of us were known by the same last name, Lewis. For years the slaves on the Lewis plantation secretly used the surname of Freedman. We vowed that if we ever ran away, we would consider ourselves a free man or woman with the surname of Freedman.

The night we ran away, a group of three women and five men, began a terrifying journey. I was one of them. Many who fled before us traveled toward Ohio, crossing the Ohio River. Our group joined the Underground Railroad on our way north through Savannah, Georgia. A safe house with a yellow light from a gas lantern in the window was a signal that beckoned us. We were muddy, drenched from rain, and very hungry, when we arrived, a ragtag group. The kind station master and his wife fed us, gave us dry clothes, and showed us to a room in the attic in case anyone came looking for runaways in the night. There was a secret door in the wall to a small space in the eves. We could hide there if someone insisted on searching the whole house.

We stayed two nights to regain our strength. I became feverish but didn't tell anyone, too terrified of being left behind. I was sure the sweating would pass.

It didn't.

The station master's wife gave each of the women, including myself a hymnal. As soon as it was dark on the third night, we left the Underground Railroad station with a map to the next station in South Carolina, and on to North Carolina and Virginia. We were given more maps at each station and told our best chance at freedom was to make our way to a state which had abolished slavery. Vermont, New Hampshire, Rhode Island, Massachusetts and Connecticut were listed, states where we would be free if we were lucky enough to get that far.

The station masters were sympathetic to our plight. All we had to do was get to one of them, or keep going to Canada, escaping the U.S. altogether.

Travel was terrifying. We couldn't hide in the forests because there were bounty hunters with dogs. The only way we could avoid capture was to go from safe house to safe house, stations on the Underground Railroad. If none, we scrambled to a river thwarting the dogs tracking on land.

Six months ago we were harbored by a station master in New Hampshire. Marshall Bradley was my savior. Seeing the yellow lantern in the window, we arrived again with mud caked clothes, and starving. I arrived sick, weak and some fever, collapsing on the floor. One of the men in my group also had a fever and chills, but he left two days later with the others, maps to Maine and on to Canada in his pocket.

My dear Marshall created a safe place for me to hide in a little house in the trees in case bounty hunters came looking for runaways. He built a trapdoor so those before me and others that followed could escape while he entertained and fed the bounty hunters and their dogs.

Many months later, when I began this journal, Marshall built a nook in the attic wall, hanging a picture over a nail concealing a little door. He wanted to give me a safe place to hide my journal, but easy enough for me to access when I wanted to write my story, my thoughts. I'm mindful that even though New Hampshire passed a law making it a free state, there are those who remain hostile, those who would happily give my name to a bounty hunter in exchange for a large sum of money.

———

GEORGIE LOOKED TO THE ceiling taking a deep breath. Holding the journal, images of the tree house, the trapdoor filled his mind. Rosemary was in this house. He could feel her fear, as if she was here with him, telling him her story.

He had to go outside, get some air, walk down to the lake. Leaving the journal on his bed, he ambled down to the water unaware that Lucas and Scooter had joined him. They romped around, lapped a little water from the edge of the lake, then settled on the leaves next to him. Absently mindedly, he stroked Scooter's silky head. "Rosemary sat beside Marshall...this very spot. What did they say to each other?"

Lucas raised his head, Scooter cocked his—both intent on Georgie talking to them.

"Rosemary was safe, no longer afraid, no longer alone. She was with Marshall."

Georgie got to his feet, hurried up the path. He had to read more of her journal. What happened to Rosemary?

Lucas broke off the path heading to his house. Scooter continued on to the big farmhouse.

Chapter 11

———

RETURNING TO THE TREE house, Georgie settled on his bed and opened the journal to the next entry.

November, 1849

So long since I've written. I was afraid to write. When I entered fresh words I immediately tore the pages out in case someone found this journal, perhaps giving it to the bounty hunters. They keep stopping at the house asking Marshall about rumors he was harboring a runaway slave. They offered him lots of money, but he always lied, keeping our secret safe. But now I feel compelled to write again.

I'm pregnant!

Marshall and I are so happy. We are filled with joy, yet fear the future.

My dear baby, I don't know if you're a girl or a boy, but I do know you came to be from the love of your father, Marshall Bradley, and his love for me, your mother, Rosemary Freedman. As I wrote in the beginning, but it bears repeating for you my little one, I first came to know your father when I was one in a group of slaves running from Atlanta. The others scattered but I remained on the farm. I was very sick but your father nursed me back to health.

Marshall was building a grand house on a hill and he asked me to stay, to help keep house. It wasn't long before we knew we were destined to be together. Such love we have for each other. My days are full, yet I fear our love will be discovered. There are still those around us who believe Coloreds should move on—certainly not marry. So, I stay on the farm, but happily so.

Marshall told me last night that he inherited some gold pieces from his father. He said he's hidden them so they wouldn't be found by the bounty hunters, said they were for our future.

My days are full keeping house, gardening, and preparing for your arrival. My need to write my story in this journal has lost its urgency, such is my contentment with this new life.

———

August, 1850

Dear baby, you're due to enter this world anytime now. I feel compelled to write in this journal again, but I fear it may be my last entry. I've not been well, sick with many complications bringing you into this world. Your birth is imminent. I'm writing this because I'm afraid I might die giving you life. If I live, then there will be many pages to follow filled with happy times.

If not, you and I will never meet.

I've put a lock of your father's hair in an envelope and a lock of my hair in another, both are tucked in the back of this journal.

If I die, your father and I have agreed that he would take you to the church in the night, leave you bundled in warm blankets in a basket so you will be safe from the storm or predators. I'm sure you won't be alone but a few hours. We trust a good family of faith will raise you. My beloved Marshall begged me not to hold him to our agreement, but I prevailed, holding him to his promise. If I wasn't a slave it would be different.

We never married. So given the nature of our union, your father will be able to marry.

———

LEANING BACK AGAINST THE headboard, Georgie visualized a newborn baby in a basket left at the church. His body shuddered. How similar to his own beginning, his dad carrying him in a basket. If it hadn't been for the Bradleys, where would he have ended up? Would he even have lived?

His eyes opened wide. He had to talk to Gran, give her the journal. As the matriarch of the family, it was a piece of the farm's history that she should have.

Entering the kitchen of the big old farmhouse, the aroma of a pot roast in the slow cooker tugged at his heart. *Had Rosemary baked such a roast in a pot swinging on the crane over the fire,* he wondered, gazing at the crane still anchored inside the fireplace with a bee-hive oven above, a precious antique today.

He found Gran in the living room, fretting over her new hobby—knitting little newborn caps for the church women's group. Scooter wanted up on her lap but the yarn tickled his ears. He finally gave up, trotting to his pillow by the fireplace. Georgie added a log to the fire.

"Got a minute, Gran? I have something for you," he said, pulling up a hassock by her rocking chair, her feet up on a little stool.

"All the time in the world. Any chance you could bring us a cup of tea? I put the teapot to steeping. It should be just right. One lump of sugar, please," she said, tucking her knitting in the side pocket of her chair.

Georgie strode to the kitchen. Returning, he set two cups of tea on the lamp table next to her chair, within easy reach for both of them.

"Now, Georgie, tell me what's on your mind." Gran took a sip of tea. She closed her eyes. "I love the blend of green tea and lemon."

"The map, Gran. I figured the marks, small circle near the big circle represented the tree house and—"

"I came to the same conclusion." Gran pulled one of the maps from her apron pocket. "Surprised you, huh? You're not the only curious one in this house. There were four in the tin box. By the way, the box is in my sewing room."

Georgie nodded, taking a sip of tea. "Earlier today I asked Finn to go on a scavenger hunt with me."

"You boys were inseparable growing up. You always watched out for Finn. He was like a younger brother. Did you two find another treasure?" Gran asked.

"Yes, in the attic. A journal, written by a runaway slave by the name of Rosemary. Rosemary comes to the farm with a group of slaves. They move on, but she is sick and remains. Marshall nurses her back to health, they fall in love. She speaks of gold pieces Marshall inherited from his father. He had hidden them, said they were for their future."

Gran stared at Georgie, her rocker still. "Do you have the journal with you?" she asked.

"Yes, right here."

Georgie removed the journal from his jacket's patch pocket, handing it to Gran. "We found this hidden behind a piece of shiplap in the attic."

Gran set her teacup down, laid the bound journal in her lap, her knarled fingers caressing the leather cover. She opened it to the first page. Her fingers running under the first few lines as she read. She paused, her eyes popping over her glasses at Georgie. "My, my, such a long time ago and now we learn of her story.

Georgie please read it to me." She handed the journal back to him.

Georgie took a sip of tea, and then read Rosemary's journal to Gran leaning back in her rocker, toe tapping the carpet, now and then pausing as Georgie turned a page.

At the end, he closed the book. "Gran, that's the last entry." Georgie flipped to the back, showed Gran the envelopes—*Marshall* written on one, *Rosemary* written on the other. Returning the envelopes inside the back cover, he handed the book to her.

Holding the soft leather to her heart, her eyes filled with tears. "Georgie, please go get Rosemary's hymnal. It's on my desk in the sewing room."

Georgie returned and read the inscription-—*To Rosemary, God speed.*

Several minutes passed, Gran leaning back in the rocker, eyes closed. "I wish my Arnie could have read this. Just think, his great, great grandfather, Marshall Bradley, a conductor on the Underground Railroad." Gran opened her eyes. "If only these walls could talk. He must have married late in life. He had a son—Arnie's great grandfather, Kenneth Bradley. So, Marshall's first love was Rosemary, and to think she died giving birth to his first child. We don't know if it was a boy or a girl. Because of the times, he left that baby at our church on the hill. I wonder what happened to the little one?"

"Gran, I've been wondering the same thing. I hope the baby had the good fortune to be accepted into a family as giving and as loving as yours—you, Jane, and Danny."

"Georgie, you and Wolfe have given this family more than you'll ever know." Gran sat up straight. Smiling she handed the journal to Georgie, but he shook his head, laying his calloused hand on top of her thin parchment skin. "It belongs to you, Gran, to the Bradleys. It's a piece of your family history."

"A treasured piece, dear. I thank you. I'll talk to Jane and Danny as to where we should display it. Now, what do you want to do with this information?"

Georgie chuckled, picked up his teacup, paced to the fireplace. "If it's okay with you, I thought I'd pay another visit to the Portsmouth library. Scour the archives for an article about a baby, probably with dark skin, left at the Lakeville church. There must have been a buzz about such a thing. We have the date—1850."

"Splendid. On Sunday I'll bring the journal to the minister, ask if there's any scuttlebutt in their archives. We have a fine puzzle in front of us, Georgie," Gran said with a twinkle in her eyes.

Chapter 12

———

THE SIXTY-SEVEN-YEAR-old man, shock of silver hair curling around his ears, stared out the window glass enclosing the atrium, across the manicured lawn to his enormous red barn. A stand of mighty maples to the right had lost their leaves, and the fall flowers had succumbed to an early frost.

Vincenzo Scarpetti was blinded by hatred. It had been several years since his son Logan had died from a bullet in Louie's Tavern down the road. The police found his charred body, burned beyond recognition from the inferno that followed a shootout. Only a piece of DNA identified the body as Logan Scarpetti.

Vincenzo Scarpetti, blamed Finn Bradley for his son's death. Vincenzo had waited, biding his time to avenge Logan's murder. Waited to settle the score, settle once and for all the feud between the Scarpettis and the Bradleys. In 1969, his father had settled with Arnold Bradley, Finn's grandfather, over a rare Picasso painting. But the settlement showed Vincenzo's father to be weak. He paid old man Bradley for the painting Logan stole from over the Bradley fireplace. In Vincenzo's mind, the Picasso rightfully belonged to the Scarpetti family in the first place. Logan had only taken what belonged to the family. The thought brought bile to his throat.

Revenge would be sweet, and he had implemented the first act of his plan.

A crystal highball glass in one hand, he held his cell to his ear with the other.

"Frankie Giovanni, my dear friend, you are well?" Vincenzo asked.

"Vincenzo Scarpetti, how I've longed to hear your voice. The years have been kind to me. You?"

"Yes, but I have much left to do. I need your help," Vincenzo said.

"Anything, anything in my power. What are you up to?" Frankie asked.

"Some old unfinished business that needs attention, needs to be resolved."

"Ah, I hear it in your voice. Bradley Farm? Am I correct?"

"You know me well, Frankie. Over the years, the Bradleys have struggled, never enough money to bring about the full glory that their land has to offer," Scarpetti said.

"But you know how, or should I say you want to take over the land, show them what fools they are? So what is your plan to eradicate this cancer in your belly?"

"I've had a plan for awhile, waiting for the right time to move. That time is upon us, my dear friend."

Chapter 13

——

IT WAS A BRISK FALL DAY. Georgie suddenly felt joyful as he strode out of the library with a copy of an article in the Penny Paper dated August 22, 1850. A baby, a newborn baby boy wailing his head off, was found a little after sunrise inside the door of the Lakeville church.

Zipping up his jacket he nodded to everyone he passed on the sidewalk, a perpetual smile spreading ear to ear. He couldn't wait to tell Gran what he'd found. But first, being Wednesday, and almost one o'clock, he was headed at a fast clip to the coffee shop on Market Street. He hoped Rosie would be there.

He checked the window as he passed to the entrance. Rosie wasn't there. Entering the café he paused letting his eyes adjust from the brilliant sunshine. He saw her sitting at a table for two against the wall on the left side. She was alone looking his way, her lips forming a half smile in recognition.

Striding over, he impulsively lifted her hand to his lips, placing a quick kiss on her soft skin.

Letting go of her hand, his smile widened. "Sorry, I didn't mean to be so forward. I'm glad to see you. Wasn't sure you'd be here. Mind if I join you?" He was a bit winded, or was he flustered at seeing the pretty woman smiling at him?

"Please, have a seat. It's nice to see you again. You seem to be walking on air. Something good happen?"

"As a matter of fact, it did. Do you like puzzles, Rosie?"

"Depends. Tell me about your puzzle."

Georgie related the story of finding a map, labeled Underground Railroad, leading him to find a journal. He told her the story written in the journal beginning in 1841, the last entry in 1850.

The waitress held a mug in the air, brows raised.

"Yes, please," Georgie said with a grin. She set the mug on the table, poured coffee and topped off Rosie's. Georgie ordered a bagel with cream cheese and chicken, then turned to Rosie. He scanned her face. Was she as glad to see him as he was excited to see her?

A waiter hustled to their table, setting his bagel order down, and quickly left.

Georgie reached for a folded piece of paper in his pocket, the copy of the article the librarian printed for him. He laid it in front of Rosie, watching her read as he bit into his bagel.

Her demeanor changed from a spark of interest to a slight furrow of her brow. Rosie laid the copy of the news article back in front of him without a comment, without looking at him.

Georgie put down his bagel, covered her hand with his. "What's the matter? It's an old article—"

"Not so old—a baby left on a doorstep, a baby not cradled in his mother's arms. An orphan. Except for the date, that could be my story."

The shudder Georgie experienced after first reading the journal jolted through his shoulders again. His fingers tightened around her hand. A simple gesture of friendship, a touchstone. Two people suddenly needing an anchor.

"Your parents…" he began, his eyes searching hers.

"Never knew them. I was an orphan, like the story in the article—a baby left on a doorstep in the middle of the night, not at a church, but an orphanage. I woke up the Sisters with my hungry wails—or so went the story I was told later. They named me Rosie because of my rosie cheeks. The head of the orphanage lived in the town of Castine, in Maine, where the orphanage was located. So I became Rosie Castine. I grew up in the orphanage—a few times I was placed in a foster home. It seemed the foster parents were only interested in the money, or they had accepted so many orphans that I proved to be one too many. Each time I was returned to the orphanage. I left at the end of high school, worked my way through nursing school. That's my story, George. What about your family?"

Air escaped in a long puff through his lips. The question of his family, or lack thereof, returned. Leaning back in the chair he pushed away his half eaten bagel.

"My dad and I live on a farm. A family farm. Not our family. The Bradley's farm. As I am told, one day my dad wandered up their driveway carrying me in a basket. I was four months old. He and I have lived on this farm ever since, in a small house on the property nestled in the woods."

"What about you mother?" Rosie asked.

"Just Dad and I. He said my mother died when I was born."

"That's it? No grandparents?" she said, waving off the waitress with a coffeepot in her hand.

"We never talk about that day he walked up the driveway. Always seemed too painful for him. So I never pushed it. You're a beautiful woman, Rosie. Have you ever been married?" Georgie asked, glancing at her bare ring finger.

"No. I grew up moving from one foster-home to another, as I said. I really didn't look for a relationship—felt I wouldn't measure up, I guess. There were a couple of times I thought it might work—a relationship with a man. Moved in with one, but I left in a week. That's one reason I turned to nursing. The patients need me, are appreciative of my help. Are you married...no ring—"

"No, came close, but it never felt right. Rosie, would you like to go out to dinner with me? Saturday? I have to get back to the farm now, but Saturday?"

"Yes, I'd like that...but Lakeville is—"

"Not that far but I'll pick you up." Georgie walked to the counter, returning with a pencil and two fresh paper napkins. "Let's trade cell numbers," he said giving Rosie a napkin. He wrote his name and cell number, handed her the pen and the napkin. She jotted down her number, sliding the napkin to him.

"Do you live close, or can I drive you home? My truck is in the city parking garage."

"I live down the street, a studio apartment in one of the old buildings."

"Are you going home? I could walk with you and then I'll know where to pick you up. Saturday, say seven? Is that good for you?"

"Yes, that's good."

They walked three blocks, only commenting on the air getting cooler. Rosie seemed lost in thought, as was he. At the entrance to her building, Georgie jammed his hands in his pant pockets. There wasn't anything more to say—no more small talk.

"I'll see you Saturday, seven. Call if you can't make it?" he said.

"Yes, you too...if you can't make it."

Chapter 14

THE DAY TURNED BLEAK, clouds scuttling in blocking the sun. Georgie wandered to the parking garage, climbed in his truck. He sat fiddling with his keys. The garage was packed, only a few people returning to their cars. The last day of October, his excitement of finding the article, of seeing Rosie, her story suddenly brought back his feeling of unease, of loss.

He didn't feel like driving home just yet. He wanted to be alone with strangers, alone with his thoughts—*Rosie left on a doorstep of an orphanage.* The image was painful. There was an underground bar around the corner. What was it Sadie and Travis liked to drink? Scotch on the rocks—that was it.

Climbing out of the truck, he ambled down the street, pulling the collar of his jacket up around his ears from a sudden gust of chilly air. It was too early for business people to be stopping off for a drink before going home, so he found the bar half empty. It was a cozy place, dim with indirect lighting, a flickering candle on each table ready to welcome the rush at five o'clock.

Hitching up on a stool by a large fish tank, Georgie ordered a Scotch, no ice.

He stared at the fish swimming aimlessly. A sudden dart by a big goldfish, gills pumping, gazed through the glass at him.

Georgie stared back.

Was God trying to tell him something—Rosie, Rosemary? Coincidence?

He didn't believe in coincidences or much else these days.

The land was real. Seasons following seasons were real. Crops sprouting in spring, leaves dropping in the fall. That he could count on. That he knew. Everything else was a mystery.

What's your puzzle? Rosie had asked him. Puzzles—a series of what ifs. A piece fit here, not there.

What if the shelves in the cellar never gave way—no map, no trap door, no journal.

No Rosie!

Rosie!

She was worth knowing.

Georgie gulped down the Scotch. Paid for his drink.

Time to head back to the farm.

———

GRAN MUST HAVE BEEN watching out the kitchen window because she popped out the back door before he crested the hill and parked. She stood waving a piece of paper at him, steadying herself with her cane.

Georgie sighed. The excitement he felt at the library and seeing Rosie was gone. Hearing Rosie's story and her questioning where she belonged in the scheme of things, weighed heavy on his heart. Climbing out of his truck, he shuffled up to Gran.

"What's the matter, Georgie? You look like you lost your best friend. Maybe my news will perk you up," she said.

Georgie reached into his pocket retrieving the copy of the news article. "I found this at the library. The Portsmouth Herald back in the day was known as the Penny Paper. I guess it only cost a penny."

Gran read the paragraph then looked at Georgie, her eyes a twinkle. "Well, I told you I was going to wait until Sunday to talk to the minister about the journal you found, but I jumped the gun. I called him this morning, shortly after you left for Portsmouth. He wasn't aware of any story about a baby being left at the church long ago, let alone a slave's baby. He made a few calls to the old timers in town. One told him where to check in the parsonage. There were several boxes with old announcements, like the programs we have today—what hymns, prayers, announcements, things like that. He found a notation dated a few days before this article you found, about a newborn baby left inside the door of the church. It seems no one knew anything about the mother, who she was, or where she came from. The baby was transported that very day to an orphanage in Exeter. Isn't that exciting? I looked to see if there were any orphanages listed in the telephone book. There was one, but what we're looking for happened so long ago it's hard to tell if it's the orphanage we're looking for. Probably not. I waited so you could make the call."

Georgie felt like he had been punched in the stomach. Another orphanage story. He shook his head. Taking the piece of paper Gran handed to him, shoving it in his pocket.

"Umm, exciting. Sorry, Gran, I can't do it right now. I have chores to do. See ya later."

He left Gran standing, her mouth agape. She turned back to the house muttering to Scooter, scooting in the door ahead of her. "What's happened to Georgie the past months—the excitement he displayed yesterday is gone? I ask you, Scooter, where is the good spirited man the family loves?"

Chapter 15

A FITFUL NIGHT, SLEEP ELUSIVE, Georgie didn't go to the farmhouse for breakfast. Sauntering down the path, he stood at the edge of the lake, the gray water reflecting off the building clouds. A cold November breeze ruffling the water, he raised his arms to the heavens. "Who the hell am I?" he yelled.

"You're my son," Wolfe said. "What's the matter with you, Georgie?"

Surprised to hear his dad's voice, Georgie reeled around, stared at the man he'd called Dad all of his life. He shook his head, his face tortured, questioning. Mouth open, gasping for breath, he let his arms dangle at his side. "So you say," he whispered.

"Your birth certificate—" Wolfe started to say, but was cut off.

"Home birth. My mother died...you told me. Her name? Betty Smith is written on the birth certificate as mother. Your name—Mr. Wolfe, father. Attending physician—blank. City—Portsmouth. How did you get it? Pay off the clerk?"

"Your birth certificate was valid enough to get your social security card. I think you're caught up in a mid-life crisis," Wolfe said, his eyes half closed to mere slits. "I hope for everyone's sake it passes soon."

"Call it what you will," Georgie replied. "Why Lakeville? Why did you walk up the Bradley's driveway?"

"Maybe serendipity? You were scrawny, sickly as a baby. Jane and Gran nursed you back to a healthy baby boy. They helped a widower who knew nothing about babies. You and I became an extended family of the Bradley's," Wolfe said. "What else needs to be known?"

Everything he had been told of his birth, which was precious little, now seemed a lie. "Who are we? Who am I?" Hands dangling at his sides, Georgie's dark eyes pierced Wolfe's.

Wolfe leaned against an old maple, plucked a piece of grass, chewed a minute as he looked at Georgie. "I grew up, as did your mother, in an orphanage. It's where we met."

Georgie looked heavenward for help. *Another orphanage story.*

Wolfe ignored his gesture. "We were given last names. I guess that's when I became known as Wolfe."

"No first name?"

"Christopher. But I've always been called Wolfe. Never told anyone my first name. Betty and I made a pact—no foster parents, no adoptive parents unless they took both of us. If anyone tried to separate us, we'd throw a tantrum until they left. We were average students at school. When we turned sixteen, we hatched a plan. In a year we'd leave the orphanage, find a job, work hard, pool our money, and when we saved enough we'd buy a house."

"Sounds like a pipedream—two kids thinking they'd conquer the world," Georgie said. Easing down to the ground covered with rotting leaves, he sat cross legged, snatched a piece of grass mimicking Wolfe. It was the first time his dad had opened up about his past.

"Yup, a pipedream, but it was our dream. When we were seventeen we left. We talked our way into jobs at a piano bar. Both washed dishes, plus worked another job bagging groceries at a supermarket. It was enough. Together we paid the rent on a room that came with a little fridge on the counter, a microwave and running water."

"The bar, didn't they question your age?"

"Sure, but we were dishwashers, agreed to work until they closed, and we were reliable. We never missed a day. We told the owner we were nineteen, soon to be twenty. He didn't care, and didn't ask for identification. So that's what we did—ran away, started a new life, a new identity. Betty became pregnant. This is where you came in. Trying to save money we took any odd jobs we could get—me a handyman, her cleaning houses. We only saved a hundred dollars, so she insisted she'd have her baby at home. She'd assisted in several births at the orphanage, also known as a place to help unwed mothers. Young girls had their babies, left them to be adopted, and returned to wherever they came from. That's the way things were done at the time—almost fifty years ago. Betty died giving birth to you."

"No doctor? No woman to help her?"

"We were a couple of scared kids, stupid kids. She was buried in a pauper's grave. I hitched a ride as far as Lakeville. I carried you in a basket. You were crying—hungry little guy. Desperate, I walked up the first driveway I came to. There you have it, my story."

"Why didn't you marry Betty?"

"No need. We lived and worked together...marriage was not in the dream—only survival."

"You wander up a driveway, Bradley Farm, ask for milk. I was four months old, or so your story goes."

"It happened." Wolfe looked away.

"Forty-six years ago—here we are."

"The Bradleys were kind. Gran and Jane—they needed help on the farm. Danny was off serving in the Army. I provided that help...yes, here we are."

"My mother—you don't even have a picture?"

"No. No picture," Wolfe said, spitting out the remains of the blade of grass.

"What did she look like? I don't look like you."

Wolfe shook his head. "You do...a little. Your mother grew into a beauty, dark olive skin like you. Black hair so shiny you swore it was thick curls of silk." Wolfe looked back at Georgie, squinting at him. "Georgie, what's this all about? Are you questioning the Bradleys welcoming us into their family? Their love? I ask you, Georgie, why now?"

"Emma at the library, Nancy my professor, and a woman at the coffee shop in Portsmouth."

"What about them?" Wolfe asked.

"Both Emma and Nancy, for no reason, asked about my family. My instant reaction was—what family? Suddenly it mattered. I had no family. No Gran. No siblings. I work hard on the farm, they pay me, but am I working to achieve something for myself? No—all for the Bradleys."

"You don't believe that. They've always treated us well—you like a son."

Georgie jumped to his feet, looked out over the water. "Like a son, but not their son." He snapped. "I stopped for coffee in Portsmouth, my first trip to the library after finding the journal. It was busy. All the tables were taken. But there was a woman sitting at a table, staring out the window. I asked if she minded if I sat in the empty chair. She nodded, then turned her head back to the window."

"Sorry, son, I don't see the connection—"

"I was sipping my coffee, reading the newspaper—checking the five-day weather forecast."

"Okay, and so..." Wolfe sighed, looked off at the lake. The water looked angry, the wind whipping up small white caps. A cold New England day—winter was approaching.

"And so, without looking at me, she asked if I was from Portsmouth. For some reason I drew a blank. When I didn't answer, she turned to see if I heard her. Stuttering, I said yes. I returned the question, asking if she was from Portsmouth."

"And what did she say?"

"For now. I found that a strange answer. Then she asked me if my family lives here too? I stumbled again, but then said yes. That was it. She turned back to the window, I returned to the weather forecast. A waitress stopped by with a pot of coffee. She addressed the woman as Rosie."

Georgie looked over his shoulder, hearing Finn.

"Georgie, Georgie, come quick," Finn yelled from the top of the hill. "Cameron said the barley's rotten."

Chapter 16

———

THE BREWERY WAS ICE COLD. Cameron Foster's face was fierce, fists clenched ready to strike. He stared at Georgie. "It's rotten. All rotten. Filled with mold. Just smell it. It's like a gym locker full of moldy towels left for weeks in a bin. The whole bucket Larry delivered this morning smells rotten." Cam spit the words at Georgie, sharp as daggers as he scooped a handful of grain from the bucket throwing it to the floor.

Georgie whirled around, stomped out of the brewery, ran up the driveway, down the path to the horse barn. Pulling out his cell as he ran, he called Larry. "I don't care where you are, Larry. Get your ass to the horse barn."

He didn't wait for a reply, shoving his cell into his shirt pocket.

The barn door was pulled back on its track. Danny stood inside holding a handful of barley grains, shaking his head.

Georgie rubbed a few grains between his fingers, threw them on the barn floor. Scowling, he charged further back in the barn to the storage area. His expression hardened as he stood next to the small pile on the floor, the last dump of barley grains. He stooped, sat on his haunches, tracing a circle in the grain with his index finger. Snapping to his feet, he traced the top of the first bin with his fingers, then scooped up a handful, then dug deeper. He moved to the second bin, the third, the fourth. He strode to the stacks of sacked grain, bagged the day after the harvest. Pulling a penknife from his pocket, he slit the bag, allowing the grain to flow onto the floor.

"Hey, Georgie, what's up?" Larry said. He was breathing hard from running through the field.

"You tell me," Georgie snapped. "The night of the harvest, did you supervise the dumping like I told you?"

"Yes, every cart."

"And oversaw the bagging the next day?"

"Yes. Why?" Larry nervously shifted from foot to foot, hands on his head.

"Who worked with you?"

"Several of the hands you asked me to call. Four guys came. A couple helped bag. What's the matter?" he asked raising his arms in front of him, palms up.

"Get me their names. Call them. Tell them to get over here ASAP. I don't care if they're working someplace else. If they ever want to work at Bradley Farm again, they'll get their butts over here. Do you hear me, Larry? Then come back. I have some questions for you and you'd better give me straight answers on why the grain we harvested is rotting."

"Rotting?"

"Something the matter with your nose, Larry? Make the calls and then get back here with the names."

"I don't know why they'd be rotting. I did everything you told me."

"Smell this." George said, pushing his hand deep under the top layer, shoving his open palm with grains under Larry's nose.

Larry pulled back at the stench, his face skewered with a sour look.

"Call the guys," Georgie snapped, pulling his cell out, tapping a number. "This is George Wolfe. I have to speak to the sheriff." Georgie glanced at Danny leaning against one of the bins watching him.

"Tom Townsend, here."

"Tommy, thank God you're in the office. I need your help. My harvest has been sabotaged—the grain stored in the barn."

"You sure, Georgie? I'll come over, but we've had rain, high humidity. Maybe—"

"I tell you it's sabotage," Georgie said, disconnecting the call.

Finn came running into the barn breathless. "Georgie, Cam said he has to cancel the two contracts from the brewery in Canada if—"

"Give me a couple of hours to check all the bags. I'll let you know. Sheriff Townsend's coming, which doesn't change the situation—mold is mold."

"Tommy's coming over? Why?"

"Why? The harvest was sabotaged, that's why."

"Okay, Georgie. Cam says this changes everything—no crop means no expansion, no upgrading the storage area with refrigeration for the hops, temperature control. He's furious. Says we'll have to use all the money we've saved to buy grain—"

"You don't have to pile it on me, Finn. I'm well aware of Cam's concerns."

"Well, okay, Georgie. I'll tell...no, I'll wait a couple of hours. See if there are any salvageable grain sacks. Good luck, bro—oh, sorry. I won't say bro again. I promise."

Georgie watched Finn make fast tracks out of the barn. Sucking in a deep breath, he turned staring at the bin. *Was everything rotting,* he wondered. Suddenly his mind turned to Rosie. He wished he was back in the coffee house, reaching across the table, holding her hand. With the stench of rotting grain, he knew he couldn't make Saturday night, but he could at least talk to her.

Retrieving his phone, he tapped her number at the top of his directory he entered last night from the napkins they traded. Her answering machine picked up.

"Hi, Rosie, it's me, George. Something's come up here on the farm. The grain I harvested has turned moldy...it's bad. I can't make it Saturday. I'll call. I hope you're doing okay. Well…have a good day. Like I said, I'll call. I…I really wanted to see you. Bye."

Chapter 17

———

DEPRESSION OR A FUNK—call it what you will. The feeling flowed over Georgie like a straight jacket and he couldn't shake it off. But deep down he knew he wasn't trying. It was almost Thanksgiving and he couldn't think of a thing to be thankful for except that he had met Rosie. He and Rosie talked on their cell phones several times. Both seemed preoccupied. Each time he didn't want to hang up, wanted to stay connected even if he couldn't hold her hand.

The farm hands, led by Larry, all pleaded innocent to mishandling the barley. They spoke with one voice—everything was fine when they left the night of the harvest, no idea how the grain started to rot. They all went straight home for some shut eye before heading to their jobs on other farms the next morning.

Sheriff Tommy Townsend came back again, listening to Georgie relate his story of that night trying to beat the storm. Only the last dump was caught in the rain. He had kept it separate as the Sheriff could see—the pile on the floor next to a bin filled with grain. Georgie said he closed the barn door and returned the combine to the farm rental yard. Sam drove him back to the farm. Larry had driven Georgie's truck during the harvest with a cart attached. Henry and Larry had tag teamed—one cart was unloaded in the barn by the farm hands while the second received the dump driving alongside the thresher.

Tommy shook his head. "Sorry, Georgie, I don't see any sign of sabotage, just a heap of bad luck with the rain."

Georgie sighed. "I think you're wrong, Sheriff. Hey, is it alright if I call you Tommy? Or, I guess it should be Sheriff. I know you played football with Finn, so you're a friend of the family and—"

"Call me, Tom. To tell you the truth, I'm a little old for Tommy."

"I hear you, Tom. But then you call me George."

They smiled at each, then glanced away.

"How did you become a sheriff?" Georgie asked.

"Well my resume goes like this. I worked part-time at a funeral home to pay my way through college. At first I wanted to be a chef—I like to eat, as you can tell," Tommy said patting his belly. "Then I took a few courses in chemistry with a minor in law. That's when I became a lawman. When did you become a farmer, or do you want to do something else?"

"I've loved being out in the field since I was a kid."

Tommy slapped his knee laughing. "I can remember coming over to play with Finn—we liked to terrify the chickens. But there you were sitting up on the tractor—"

"Sure 'nuff I was twelve. At that age, every year there's a big change in a kid."

"Twelve? You looked twenty," Tommy said.

"Only five years older than you and Finn. The twins, Sadie and Marshall, were born just after my dad and I called the tree house home. Do you have kids, Tom?"

"Naw. Married once, but when I became a cop, she couldn't take the stress. We divorced."

"That's too bad. Hey, did Finn tell you about the maps and the journal we found?"

"Yes. I stopped by to have a beer a few days ago. You were in Portsmouth. That was something else—you two crawling around under the tree house. Well, it's been nice chatting with you, George, but duty calls. Tell you what, get me a paper bag. I'll take some of the grain into the lab for analysis. Would that make you feel better?"

"Hold on a second. There's a brown lunch sack in Danny's workshop."

Georgie quickly got the lunch sack, stuck his hand deep under the top layer of grain, and put a fist full in the bag.

Tommy patted him on the shoulder. "Call me if you find any evidence to go along with your suspicions."

"Will do, and thanks for coming over."

Georgie watched the squad car roll down the driveway. *No sabotage?* "Well I don't buy it," he mumbled, turning back into the barn. "Something happened here." The mold in the sacks wasn't bad, but, unfortunately, not bad wasn't good.

He walked to the front of the barn, then foot by foot around the perimeter, eyes scanning from floor to ceiling, back to the floor. Nothing caught his attention. Danny and Wolfe joined him. Georgie told them that Tommy had been here and he didn't think it was sabotage.

"Sabotage or not, Cameron and Finn are trying to figure out how they're going to stay in business until January," Danny said. "They're looking at a month and a half of holidays which are always big for the pub. Finn said they doubted they had enough beer on hand to last through New Year's Eve. They're going to have to buy more malted barley if they decide to start brewing the day after Thanksgiving."

Thinking of the holidays reminded Georgie of Rosie. He hadn't called in a few days while coping with the ramifications of the grain turning moldy. Slapping his hat on his head, he left Danny and his dad in the workshop corner of the horse barn and walked down toward the lake.

He tapped Rosie, number one in his cell directory. She picked up on the first ring.

"Rosie, it's George. I can't tell you how sorry—"

"Hey, don't worry. I've been pulled onto extra shifts."

"What happened?"

"There was a big pile up on the bridge over the river to Maine, to Kittery. A bus of seniors was returning from a weekend at the Foxboro casino in Massachusetts. I still have patients who were caught in the wreckage. I'm glad you called."

"Look, it's almost Thanksgiving. How about I come pick you up and you join the Bradleys and me for a big old turkey dinner on the farm? Would you like that?"

"Yes, I would. I've put in enough overtime, I'm sure I can finagle the day off or put in for the night shift. But you don't have to pick me up. Can you send me directions? From what you said, it sounds like a straight shot from Portsmouth. To tell you the truth, I'd like a drive in the country, clear my head from the smell of antiseptic."

"Sounds great. I'll email you a map, annotated by yours truly. Rosie, it's really nice to hear your voice. I miss you."

Chapter 18

PREPARATIONS WERE IN FULL swing for tomorrow's Thanksgiving feast. The aroma of baking bread escaped the beehive oven in the stone fireplace. A low flame flickered in the hearth. A kettle, simmering chicken broth with carrots, parsnips, and herbs, hung on the iron crane. The broth would be stirred into the turkey dressing and the mashed potatoes. Sometimes it was sipped, giving the cooks a boost between chopping celery, walnuts, and breaking up pieces of toasted bread.

Gran sat in her rocker snapping beans for the onion, cheese and bean casserole. Jane kept an eye out the kitchen window for Sadie and her husband Travis. They were due any minute from their home in Washington D.C. Marshall, Sadie's twin brother, would be missing this year. He was in Tel Aviv with his fiancée Anna. Jeli would also be missing. She remained in China trying to put together a furniture deal.

Danny had reported to Gran, that the men on the farm were gathered around a table in the pub—Danny and Wolfe sitting silently, listening to the conversation, sometimes heated between Finn, Cameron and Georgie. Danny told her that no matter how they figured the business, they still came up short either on the quantity of grain needed to keep the pub open through the holidays, or how best to portion out the money, which was precious little, to creditors. Gran relayed Danny's message to Jane and the women of the farm preparing the feast.

Katie and Daisy, Finn and Katie's adopted daughter along with Carrie, were in the kitchen helping with the pies, or whatever Gran and Jane needed. With the turn of events, losing the barley crop, there was no mention of Rosemary's journal, or the Underground Railroad maps. They were no longer the topic of conversation.

The women were doing their darndest to keep the chatter light, praying the brewpub's plight would somehow be resolved, but they were at a loss as to how that would come about.

Jane was anxious to see her daughter. Sadie, always pragmatic, was also capable of finding a silver lining in a situation. She wished her youngest daughter Jeli would surprise them by returning home early from China. Jeli could make anyone laugh, and right now the family could use a dose of levity.

"They're here. Sadie's here," Jane called out. Jane wiped her hands on her white bib apron as she dashed out to help Sadie carry in jars of her special cranberry-orange chutney.

Jane gave Sadie a big hug, followed by Daisy out the door on Jane's heels. Travis opened the back of the large black SUV. He gave Jane a peck on the cheek, then tucked two small overnight cases under his arms.

"Good heavens, Travis—such a big car?"

"Only vehicle available unless we wanted to wait an hour. We didn't," he said chuckling. "I'll take these cases upstairs. Same bedroom?" he asked.

"Yes, and the men are down at the pub. Talking about the harvest—"

"Sadie told me. I'll go down. Anything you need, Jane?"

"No, all set here. Oh, just so you two know, Georgie told us this morning that he's invited a friend to dinner tomorrow," Jane said.

"A female friend?" Sadie asked.

"Yes. Her name is Rosie."

"Anything serious going on?" Travis asked.

"I don't know. She's a nurse, works at a hospital in Portsmouth. That's all I know."

"I'd like to see the journal Georgie found. I did a paper in high school on the Underground Railroad," Travis said.

"The journal was all we could talk about until, you know, the barley grain issue. I thought we'd have a light dinner tonight before, you know, the big dinner—fried chicken, salad and, of course, cupcakes that Daisy baked up," Jane said.

Sadie was already in the kitchen in a discussion with Carrie and Katie. The two, their husbands who are partners in the brewpub, were obviously worried about the business going under.

Chapter 19

———

Thanksgiving

STANDING AT THE TOP of the driveway, Georgie's eyes were fixed on the road. Rosie had just called and was minutes away. He told her to watch for the Bradley Farm sign. "It's big, on your right. You can't miss it," he said, his heart skipping a beat. Within a couple of minutes, her white Chevy coupe purred up the driveway parking where he flagged to park. Opening her car door, he extended his hand, pulling her into a quick hug and a peck on her cheek. She was dressed in her signature black boot-cut slacks, white cable knit sweater and silver hoop earrings. Smiling, he grasped her hand as Finn, Katie, and Daisy run up.

The introduction was short as the family filed out of the house, laughing and enthusiastically welcoming Rosie to the farm. Georgie stood by her side, keeping hold of her hand as Sadie took over introducing Gran, Pops, and Jane.

Travis nudged in front of them all. "Nice to meet you, Rosie. I'm married to Sadie, and we're all pretty harmless unless it's a battle for the last chocolate chip cookie. Then, it's every gal or guy for himself," he said, giving Rosie a hug. Everyone commenced to talk at once, Gran leading the parade back into the house.

"Dinner's ready but let's take a minute, have a glass of wine," Jane said. "Wolfe, will you put another log on the fire in the living room?"

"You bet, added more logs to the bucket this morning," Wolfe said.

"Trav and I will see to the wine," Sadie said. "You all go on, enjoy the fire."

In the living room, Danny settled himself next to Rosie on the couch, Jane on the other side. Georgie sat in a chair facing Gran in her rocker. He couldn't take his eyes off Rosie. She was prettier than ever, their eyes continually seeking each other out. After dinner he planned to show her around the farm. He was happy how the family embraced her, and dinner was going to be nice, but he was anxious to have some time alone with her as well.

———

EVERYONE WAS SEATED AROUND the long harvest table, heads bowed as Pops said grace. Rosie sat between Georgie and Wolfe. Gran, all spiffed up in her favorite red-plaid wool skirt, white shirt-waist blouse, gazed around at the family and their friends. A smile played on her lips. Daisy hustled back and forth to the counter, finally sitting still with a turkey drumstick.

They passed bowls of potatoes, mashed and sweet, the green bean casserole and platters of white and dark meat. The silverware was the only sound—knives and forks against china plates, china passed down from generations of Bradleys, as far back as the first Marshall Bradley. The men, under Gran's dress code for a major holiday, acquiesced to her wishes, giving their jeans and t-shirts a rest—shirts, trousers, tie optional, no sneakers.

It was a strained silence, silence portending gloom and doom until Travis had enough. He nudged Sadie's arm. She glanced at him. He nodded. She picked up her dessert fork, tapped her wine glass.

"Attention everyone. Travis and I have been batting around ideas on where the gold pieces could possibly be hidden, the ones mentioned in Rosemary's journal. Gran read the paragraph to us over the phone the day you found the journal, Georgie. Travis and I thought it might be fun to explore hiding places. What do you say, Georgie? A good idea? Might be fun? I for one have to walk around to make room for those pies lined up on the hunter's hutch."

"Sure, Sadie. Things have been a little hectic around here. Forgot about the journal," Pops said.

"Good, but first, Travis and I have a surprise for you, Pops and mom, and Gran, and Wolfe."

"Me?" Wolfe said with a chuckle.

Sadie smiled. The starch in everyone's collars had softened.

"Marshall and I have had several conversations, and Anna agreed with our surprise. Wait just a minute while I get something from my purse. Katie, will you pour everyone a cup of coffee?"

Daisy's eyes sparkled. "I'll help too, Aunt Sadie," the young girl said popping up from her chair.

Lucas and Scooter lifted their heads, watched the sudden activity, then went back to sleep on their doggie blankets by the fire.

Sadie returned with a zippered pouch. Taking her seat, she balanced the pouch on the table between her fingers, taunting her audience. "Marshall and Anna have invited us, Gran, Pops, mom, Wolfe, along with Travis and me, to come for a visit to Tel Aviv—to celebrate Hanukkah and Christmas. The two happen to be within four days of each other this year."

Jane and Danny gasped, her hand reaching for his as she straightened the lace collar on her practical brown-wool dress. The dress was topped with a white cardigan that could be shrugged off when the pace of getting the feast to the table turned stressful.

"I hardly think I can—" Gran started to say.

"Marshall and I knew you might have reservations. So Travis and I are going to escort you. Thing is, Marshall got a fantastic deal on plane tickets out of Boston. Don't even try to come up with excuses on why you can't go."

"In three weeks?" Jane whispered.

"Yes. So, after we explore for gold, give it an hour, we'll finalize our plans. Katie, can you and Carrie clean up the kitchen after dessert so Travis and I can help everyone with their lists, answer questions?"

"Of course, and the trip sounds like a grand adventure," Carrie said.

"I can help, Mommy," Daisy said jumping to her feet again, starting to clear the plates.

"I'd love to help too, Rosie said. "It's the least I can do after this wonderful dinner."

"Wait," Gran said waving her hand. "We can't possibly get a passport that fast."

"It's tight, Gran. You'll send in the form tomorrow morning for a visitor's visa. Travis has it all set up with a friend of his. He's expecting the paperwork from all of you. Travis and I already have our passports so we'll gather what you need tonight, fill out the forms in the morning before Trav and I leave for Washington. Now, I'm ready for the gold rush. Georgie, you lead the exploration," Sadie said smiling. The news of the surprise trip was received better than she thought.

Georgie looked to the ceiling shaking off a smart remark. "Finn and I scoured the tree house when we found the journal. The gold could be anywhere. The brewpub barn was essentially gutted when Finn and Cam renovated so skip that. Maybe we should split up—the farmhouse, the barn by the road, and the horse barn. I pretty much gutted the horse barn—tore out the stalls replacing them with storage bins for the barley and made space for the installation of the refrigeration units for the hops, whenever there's money."

"Good idea. We'll split up. Everyone have their cell phones? If one of us discovers something, we call," Travis added.

"Well, given the first Marshall Bradley was rumored to have been into racehorses, kinda like my dad," Pops said, "I'd like to start in the horse barn, my workshop. You didn't do any *gutting* there, Georgie."

"All right, then maybe we women will check the walls, the floors, under the staircases, for a secret hiding place here in the house," Sadie said. "We emptied the attic back to the studs long ago, so I think we can eliminate that. Better yet, we'll leave the attic and the antique shop in the front barn for when we get back from Tel Aviv. Look in the daylight."

"Rosie, how about you come with me and Danny?" Georgie said.

Rosie nodded. "Sounds fun. Fine with you, Mr. Bradley?"

"You bet, Rosie," Danny said.

"It's a plan. One hour," Sadie said. "If we come up empty, we meet back here in the kitchen for pie—I have first dibs on the pecan."

"Hey, that's my favorite," Finn said, a pout on his lips.

"Too bad little brother. I spoke first."

"You boys going outside better bundle up," Gran said. "Rosie, my red scarf is on a peg at the back door."

"Thanks, Mrs. Bradley. I'll find it."

"Please, dear, call me Gran."

Chapter 20

SPLITTING INTO TWO GROUPS, Travis winked at Sadie as he shoved his arms through the sleeves of his coat. Sadie leaned close. "You certainly know how to liven up a party," she whispered planting a kiss on her husband's cheek.

Gran said she'd sit by the fire until Sadie's group was ready to search the first floor. She'd supervise the investigation from her rocker. Sadie led the ladies upstairs to the third floor—Daisy darting into Jeli's bedroom, Lucas and Scooter jumping up on her bed.

Pops topped off his coffee mug, handing it to Wolfe to carry. With one hand on his cane, the other woven through Wolfe's free arm for support, the pair ambled down the path to the horse barn behind the younger men. In the cool air of night, his stump was giving him fits, but he didn't complain. He was happy to be part of the adventure. He smiled, noting up ahead Georgie held Rosie's hand.

Finn and Cameron decided to have another look at the storage area Georgie had built. Finn didn't think they'd find the gold, but in repurposing the barn, Georgie wasn't exactly looking for gold.

As Pops slid onto the seat of his favorite rocking chair, he reached for his coffee cup that Wolfe held. This corner of the horse barn was his wood working shop—a lathe, a workbench with rows of small clamps, bottle caps screwed to the underside of shelves, bottles holding nails, screws, washers, to name a few items. In the beginning, the first Marshall Bradley had used this area as a tack room. Now, the cozy nook was definitely a man cave. The original pot belly stove kept Pops warm in the winter.

Nowadays in his late sixties, he and Wolfe could be found puffing on their pipes while solving problems around the world.

Letting the young bucks check the walls for secret compartments, Pops called out to Wolfe, "Try that next board. It looks loose to me."

Pops kept scanning the small paintings hanging on the wall across from where he was rocking. It had been a long time since he had really looked at them. Bradley Senior, being a horseman, had collected an array of paintings. Most were done in oil, signed with the name of the stallion, the mare, the filly or colt written on the back.

Getting to his feet, Pops continued to scan the paintings. His eyes slowly moved from one to the other. Eyes pinched, he paused on a painting of a golden stallion. "Wolfe, hand me that painting, will you?" Pops said, pointing to the gold stallion, as he sat back down on his rocker.

"Which one?" Wolfe asked.

"The one on the left, biggest one," Pops said.

Wolfe lifted the painting off the square iron nail, handing it to Pops.

Pops turned it over. "Give me a flathead screwdriver, will ya?"

"Here, how's this one? Small enough to get under those little nails?"

"Yup," Pops said as he loosened the nails, putting them in Wolfe's palm. The nails removed, he used the screwdriver to loosen them, then lifted the rough-hewn thin board securing the painting in the frame.

"Now, would you look at this—an envelope, certainly old." Pops opened the flap and carefully removed the folded paper inside. "Hey, it's a letter written by my great, great grandfather. Finn, come here. It's signed, Marshall Bradley, December 9, 1880."

"Read it, Pops," Finn said.

———

To my dear Rosemary. I will be seeing you soon. I miss you so. I've had a full life and at seventy, I'm ready to leave. A young widow lady entered my life soon after you died. She didn't know why, but she saw I was in a deep depression. Helping me back from that dark place, she said she loved me. She also said she knew that I must have found true love before and lost it. She understood if I didn't feel the same about her. We married and we had a son. Kenneth is a good man. He will inherit Bradley Farm.

My dearest Rosemary, I felt such anguish when you left me. I wanted to end my life, join you. To this day I wish I had kept our son. I'm going to put this letter behind the painting of my favorite steed, Gold Bullion. You always said he was the most beautiful animal you had ever seen.

Prejudice remains around me in Lakeville because I was a station master for the Underground Railroad, and I don't want to cloud Kenneth's chances to keep the farm going. So, I'm putting this letter behind Bullion's painting. Hopefully, some grandson or daughter down the line will find it.

My father was a wealthy land owner in England, and I was lucky to inherit his wealth, enough to buy the farm, build our farmhouse, dear Rosemary. With the inheritance I purchased Bullion as a colt and raised him to be a champion. My father procured five gold bars in London. I sold two of the bars to pay for the farm and build our house. One bar weighed 275 ounces, a heft of seventeen pounds. I was able to sell the two for a little more than $10,000. A princely sum to start my life on the farm. I mention the value only to let my heirs down the line, the one who finds this letter, know the worth.

I have tucked the three remaining bars under the shiplap boards behind Bullion's painting. Should the painting be sold at auction along the way, then the gold will remain hidden for many generations, hidden as our baby's life remains a mystery to me. This is a mystery that haunts me with every beat of my heart.

Kenneth has been successful in building a business out of farming so he doesn't need the gold bars I showed you, that came with my inheritance.

My beloved Rosemary, if only I could give the gold I've saved from Bullion's racing success and stud fees, adding to my father's estate, to our baby boy. I once tried to find him, but hit a wall at an orphanage. And so my darling Rosemary, I will sign this letter, hide it in the frame behind Bullion's picture.

Dearest Rosemary, I hope and pray I will join you soon. I can hear your gentle laugh, feel your touch. In the eyes of God, you and I are one.

Your beloved Marshall.

Chapter 21

———

RUNNING TO THE TOOL ROOM, leaving everyone staring at the letter in Pop's hand, Georgie returned with a crowbar and a hammer. He carefully inserted the curved end of the bar in the crack of the vertical shiplap where the painting had hung. The board popped out revealing a cavity between the studs. At the floor level was wedged a very rusty metal container the size of a shoebox. Bending down to lift the container, he was surprised at how heavy it was. Applying more muscle, he lifted the rusty box out of the hiding place, setting it with a thump on the floor in front of Pops.

"He wrote in the letter it was about fifty pounds," Pops whispered.

No padlock was attached to the loop. Georgie lifted the lid which fell backward to the floor, breaking away from the rusty hinges. The men circled around, looked down at three gold bars. Rosie stood back wide eyed.

Travis bent over on his haunches, lifted a bar, pumping a couple of times checking the weight. Pulling out his phone, he took a picture, immediately sending it to his partner at the FBI noting the ounces indicated in the letter, the age, and that the bar was purchased in London around 1840. He asked the agent to relay back what he found, today's value, ASAP. He stood holding his cell, waiting. Then he called Sadie. "Found the gold. Come on down to the horse barn."

Travis looked at Georgie who as looking at him.

"How much? Dollars?" Georgie asked, his voice barely audible.

"Close to a million," Travis said.

"A million?" Finn said. His voice hushed, fingers laced behind his neck, jaw dropping.

Everyone kept their gaze on the metal box, trying to process what they had just found.

"We're here? What did you find?" Sadie called out as she, Gran, and the others including Daisy and the dogs, rounded the corner. They looked at the men's faces, following their gaze to the rusty old box on the floor.

"A million, Sadie," Finn said.

"A million, like in dollars?" Jane said squeezing in alongside her son.

"I think this calls for a celebration," Pops said. "Anybody know where a guy can get a cold beer?"

"Good idea, Pops," Finn said. "What do we do with...with the gold?"

"Well, it was safe for more than a hundred years where we found it. I say you put her back, board her up, and hang Bullion back on the nail." Pops said. "Travis, take a couple more pictures of the bars and the letter. Be sure to get the markings on the bars. Do your research and tell us how much the bars are really worth. I think it best we not talk about what we found. Maybe it's fool's gold. In any event, we can dream. Now, let's celebrate."

"Sounds good, Pops. A beer and then back to the house. Don't forget you have visa forms to fill out," Sadie said.

After the lights lit up the brewpub and the open sign on the front door, Finn put out a call to a couple of the regulars to pass the word along, come on down to the pub. They were open for a few rounds to finish off the Thanksgiving holiday and to gear up for black Friday.

Gradually the regulars, then passersby looking for a place to watch another football game, came strolling in, filling the pub with chatter and laughter.

Finn sidled up to Danny. "Pops, what made you pick that painting?"

"Easy. I knew from stories passed down from my grandfather, that the gold horse was my ancestor Marshall's favorite and that he named him Bullion," Pops said with a wink and a thumbs up signal.

"Nothing gets by you, Pops." Finn hugged his dad. He saw Cameron adjusting one of the taps behind the bar, and ambled over.

Finn grinned at Cameron. "Maybe we'll live to brew another day, partner," he said.

"You think?" Cam said, doubt in his scrunched brows.

"I don't think. I know. Pops flashed me a thumbs up."

Daisy flitted around like a firefly, filling the pretzel bowls as the new arrivals ordered glasses, bottles, or pints of beer.

"Hey, little girl," one of the patrons called out helping himself to a handful of pretzels. "You and that bartender seem pretty happy tonight—gave my beer with an extra head of foam. You had a nice Thanksgiving?"

"Oh, yes. The bartender is my daddy. We found a pot of gold, like the Leprechaun in my storybook. Millions and millions."

"Really? Where did the Leprechaun find this pot of gold, at the end of a rainbow?" the man said laughing.

"In my grandpa's workshop, behind a golden horse," she whispered, giggling as she refreshed the bowl of pretzels, twirling about in her pink, Cinderella princess dress. Her pigtails, tied at the end with pink bows, flaring out.

There was a commotion by the bar as Finn donned his cowboy hat, and Sadie, in a bright, long-sleeve red dress, pulled out a couple of bar stools and their guitars. Strumming a few cords, they launched into a piece of line dance music, extra hot. The patrons began slapping their thighs, boots stomping on the floor, pulling back the tables.

Sheriff Townsend strolled in, tapped Georgie on the shoulder. "Come with me," he said.

"I'll be right back, Rosie," Georgie said.

"Okay," she replied, clapping in rhythm as the line moved forward.

Tommy and Georgie walked to the side of the pub. Georgie leaned back against the wall listening to Tommy, straining to hear what he was saying over the ruckus behind him.

"I didn't want to alarm Finn, but I did some checking. Nothing really turned up. However, I came across some information. Maybe relevant, or maybe not."

"What?"

"Finn's partner—"

"Cameron?" Georgie asked.

"Seems he took out an insurance policy on the brewery, business insurance. He's the only one listed as a beneficiary in case of bankruptcy."

"I'll talk to Finn. Thanks. As you say, it's probably nothing. Maybe Finn took out a policy as well—"

"Not that I found," Tommy said.

"Hey, Mom, Pops, I'm home," Jeli shouted, her mop of red curls bouncing as she ran in the door.

Finn and Sadie kept playing as the family circled around Jeli, hugging, whispering like they were imparting a mystery. Her red curls sparked hearing the news of the gold bars and the surprise trip to Tel Aviv.

"Oh, I want to go too. I'll check with Sadie and get the same flight or close to it," Jeli said, giving Pops a kiss. Laughing, she pulled her phone from her tote and merrily ran through the crowd taking pictures. She grabbed Cam's arm, asking him to take a picture of the family when Finn and Sadie took a break—before the next number. He nodded, and Jeli pulled all the family members plus Rosie, around Gran when the music stopped.

Pictures taken, Sadie and Finn returned to their barstools, plus a third stool for Jeli, picking up the beat where they left off. Retrieving her guitar from a shelf behind the bar, Jeli joined them.

Georgie picked up Rosie's hand. "How about a dance so I don't get teased by Finn tomorrow, and then you and I can take a walk?"

Rosie nodded her head. "I have to be going soon."

Georgie drew her into his arms. She fit just right.

The pub was hopping, many planning outrageous strategies for a Black Friday shopping spree as they passed around pitchers of beer.

Chapter 22

IT WAS TEN O'CLOCK and the pub was rocking, but Georgie was anxious to be alone with Rosie. Even with the excitement of finding the gold bars, he found it hard to keep his eyes from wandering to her. Taking Rosie's hand, he nodded toward the door grabbing their coats off the chairs.

A full moon lit the path up the hill as if it was day. Georgie hunched in his jacket, hands stuffed in his pockets.

"Thanks for coming, Rosie. I hope you had a good time...meeting the Bradleys."

"They're a wonderful family, George. I don't know why you keep saying they're great but always adding that they're not your family, or Finn is not your brother. From what I saw, they consider you family even if you don't. Your dad is quiet, but certainly feels at home. He dotes on Danny."

"Yep, he does. When Danny came home from the hospital with a prosthetic leg, he was suffering from depression. Dad saw to his care. It was his idea to retrofit the tack room in the horse barn with woodworking tools. Danny loved it. Snapped him out of his depression."

"The gold...I've never seen anything like it...all those years behind that board."

"Me either. Finn and Cam were headed for bankruptcy. I think I told you about the crop failure. Well, not a failure. Bad luck with the storm."

"Do you still think it was sabotage?"

"I'm sure of it but can't prove it. There's the tree house up ahead. Dad renovated it so we could live there. Gran and Jane supplied the materials."

"As I said, they look at you as family."

"Well, I'm not." Georgie grasped Rosie's hand, twirled her into his arms, tentatively touching his lips to hers. When she didn't resist, he kissed her again. His breathing hitched. He stepped back.

"Sorry...I've wanted to kiss you since you slid out of your car," he said with a smile, giving her cheek a peck. "Let's go sit by the lake. Can you stay a little longer?"

Rosie put her hand on his arm, her fingers reaching up, touched his cheek turning his face to her.

"George, I'm not sorry you kissed me." She put her hands on his chest, on tip toe, her hands circling his neck, she gently bent his head to her and softly, lingeringly, kissed him back. "Don't feel you have to apologize for your feelings. I haven't known you very long, but I can tell you are kind, work hard, and for some reason you question everything around you. Why is that?"

Sighing, he stuffed his hands back in his pockets, accepting Rosie fishing her arm through his as they walked in silence to the lake. Sitting on the bench in the moonlight, the lake calm, shadows from the trees across the way dancing on the water, Georgie frowned. He bent forward, elbows on his thighs, the toe of his boot digging at the grass.

"I feel lost, Rosie. Why now? I keep asking myself that. All of a sudden my life, going forward, I see nothing but empty pages. Don't get me wrong. I love farming. The miracle of seedlings breaching the rich soil, the miracle of life as they reach for the sun."

Rosie said nothing, snuggling closer to his side.

He turned, his face drawn, sadness in his eyes. "You and I have much in common. We didn't know our mothers. At least I have my dad. The first time I saw you in the coffee shop, staring out the window, you looked like what I was feeling—lost."

"I remember. It had been a bad day…I did feel lost. You love the land, and like you I love…I take great comfort in helping my patients. But there are times I feel very alone, like that day we happened to meet."

"Maybe we didn't just happen to meet—like my dad walking up the driveway of this farm, the Bradleys becoming a make-believe family."

"I don't know, George. I'm not much of a fatalist, not much of a believer in chance meetings being anything more than that…an empty chair on an otherwise busy afternoon."

"Hmmm me either…I guess," he said.

Rosie shivered. "I have to go. I'm on duty in a few hours. Price I had to pay for taking Thanksgiving off—happily paid," she said squeezing his hand."

They stood, ambled up the path to her car, his arm casually draped around her shoulders.

"George, thanks for inviting me to Thanksgiving dinner. I loved every minute. The Bradleys are so kind, but you really didn't have to provide a treasure hunt—that was over the top," Rosie said with a giggle.

"Yep, that was over the top. How about dinner next week?"

"Let me check my shift schedule."

"Okay, I'll text…no, I'll call you. Rosie, it meant a lot to me…your being here today."

Georgie kissed her forehead then opened the car door. About to slide in behind the wheel, she turned into his arms, hands on his shoulders, and again on tip toe, gently brushed his lips with hers. Climbing into the car, she smiled as he closed the door.

A sudden chill ran up his spine as her car rolled down the driveway. He wished she was still in his arms. Did she feel the same, he wondered pulling out his phone. He wanted to hear her voice, her laugh. He closed the phone. She'd think he was being forward—a kiss, that's all, just a kiss.

He sighed. No, it was much more. He'd call her soon.

Georgie stood at the top of the driveway watching the taillights of her car until she turned left on to the road, disappearing from his sight.

Chapter 23

JUST BEFORE MIDNIGHT ON Thanksgiving, the Emergency Room check-in desk at the Portsmouth hospital repeatedly called for assistance as to which walk-in should be seen next—car accidents, cuts from being overzealous carving a turkey, and trip-and-fall mishaps were common.

Rosie floated from the ER to the OR. When she was not needed in the OR, she was assigned patients with cuts and bruises, sending the patient home bandaged, or asking them to wait for the doctor to see them.

Rosie kept her focus on each patient, but when she had time to take a breath, her mind filled with images of George and the Bradley family. She was shocked at the warmth that flowed through her body, heart beating faster—George's tentative kiss, waiting to see if she responded.

Responded?

If she recollected the moment right, she kissed him back, and again with one last kiss before slipping into her car.

"Nurse, are you okay?" the patient whispered. The fifty-something woman suffered a burned hand draining a pot of potatoes.

"Oh yes, I'm fine," Rosie said. "Is your bandage too tight?"

"No dear. I was remembering when I had that look—new love?"

"Oh, I don't...yes, a new love. Heady stuff," Rosie said.

"Yes, it is. Don't let it get away," the woman said, smiling as she left.

The woman was Rosie's last patient. Was it a lull? Rosie wanted to take advantage of the empty ER, wanted to be alone with her thoughts. She let the check-in attendant know that she was going outside for a breath of air. Stopping at the staff kitchen, she poured a cup of coffee and then stepped outside.

It was a beautiful crisp night. The stars sparkled as she walked to her car. Sliding in, she sipped her coffee, then laid her head back. She was in love. It happened with such force she could hardly breathe.

Rosie didn't question how she knew, she simply knew she loved the farmer with all her heart. But did he feel the same? Did she dare let herself believe he felt the same? Imagine being with him when they fell asleep at night, being in his arms when she woke in the morning? The woman said not to let it slip away.

Oh no, she knew what the lack of a family was like. At the orphanage, no matter how much they tried, it wasn't the same as what she witnessed sitting at the Thanksgiving table with the Bradleys. Every time she snuck a peek at George, he was looking at her and that was before they kissed.

The thrill of the treasure hunt ending with the revelation of the letter was, in Rosie's mind, more precious than the gold. Was the love she felt for George the same as how Rosemary described in her journal, and Marshall Bradley's letter, waiting for death to release him to be with Rosemary again?

If she and George said their vows to be together for the rest of their lives—yes, it would be like that. She knew it in her heart.

A siren pierced her thoughts. It was coming close. Finishing the last of her coffee, Rosie, warmed by her thoughts of George and the day with him, hurried back to the ER—time to attend to a new patient.

Chapter 24

THE DAYS WERE GROWING COLDER. An early frost, perhaps snow flurries were touted in the weather report. Scarpetti was almost giddy as he watched the report on television. The sooner winter arrived, the sooner spring would come. He had to be ready. There was still much to be done to continue with his plan. It was time to talk to Frankie, time to let him know about their glorious future, once again in business together.

It was also time for a little cognac as he laid out the scope of the business deal he was proposing. Pouring the rich amber liquid into the crystal cordial, he rang Frankie.

"Ah, Vincenzo, I was hoping you would call. How was your thanksgiving my friend?"

"Superb. The family just left for Florida. And you, Frankie, how was your holiday?"

"Very nice. I hope you're calling about our future partnership regarding Bradley Farm?"

"Yes. Actually, I have taken a small step. I do believe the brewpub Finn Bradley opened was a good idea, and growing crops for malt barley to establish their brand of craft beer was genius. Frankie, it was not the genius of the Bradleys, but of a man who joined Finn as the brewmaster. I'm not sure you are aware that barley and hops grown in different parts of the country produces a unique taste. So, a brewery in Arizona, for instance, has a distinct flavor even if the same brewing process is used. Barley and hops grown in New England will be purchased, sought after, by breweries in other states. Then they can sell their own specialty beer that the local competition can't match unless they import the raw ingredients from us."

"Ah, I see where you're going, my dear friend."

"But that's just the tip of my plan," Scarpetti said.

"The tip of your plan? Tell me, what else are we going to do?"

"Well, along comes my state of New Hampshire. She is considering to join her sister states in passing a law to make marijuana legal for adult recreation. The land around Bradley farm is a forest for the most part and could be cleared. You couple that land with my thousand acres spread, and I will be able to provide not only the best craft beer, but with your help, be a major supplier of pot to all of New England."

Scarpetti paused, taking a sip of his Cognac. "Now picture this, Frankie. I'll create a private club in my new pub for patrons looking to enjoy a little weed before they leave."

"Oh, my dear, dear Scarpetti, you make me feel young again. I presume you would look to my family to once again be a distributor of your products?"

"Sole distributor, Frankie. There is one problem in my plan."

"What's that, Vincenzo?"

"Finn Bradley."

"Ah, the man responsible for your son's untimely death. Even if indirectly, he let it happen. But what is the problem, Vincenzo?"

"By luck of mother nature, and a nudge from my family, the brewpub's barley crop, shall we say, is unusable as it lay rotting in their barn."

"That should not be a problem, Vincenzo. Tell me the real problem," Frankie urged.

"The first Marshall Bradley, way back in 1840—he's the problem, unless we turn it to our advantage."

"Ah, the beginning of the feud between your family and his," Giovanni said.

"Yes, great, great grandfather Scarpetti wanted the land but Bradley scooped it up from under his nose. Seemed he out bid my family—which will not happen again."

"How so?" Giovanni asked.

"Seems the Senior Bradley left some gold, let me restate that, hid some gold in the old horse barn for future generations of Bradleys. It was recently uncovered."

"Tell me you have it?" Giovanni said with a chuckle.

"Not yet, but I'm working on it. Not only will the Bradleys have to declare bankruptcy, they will be forced to sell, to leave their precious farm," Vincenzo said.

"And you will purchase the property at a sale price with their own gold—a despicable, lovely plan indeed. Besides sole distributor of your produce and beer, let me know what my family can do to help our partnership along," Giovanni said.

"Two things, my dear friend. I may need a little muscle. Two men will be contacting you for the job. Second, I need someone who can make sure a certain person will join with my family."

"You are a devil, Vincenzo. Tell me one thing," Giovanni said.

"And what is that, dear friend."

"How did you learn about the hidden gold mine?"

"From a baby butterfly, you might say."

Chapter 25

IT HAD BEEN THREE WEEKS since Georgie had seen Rosie, but it seemed like three years. Finn and Cam kept him busy with questions. Questions about expanding the horse barn storage capabilities, whether to clear more land to produce more barley and hops, the best way to set up the whole operation to market the crops to other breweries?

But that was then.

It was Saturday night, and he had a date with Rosie. He felt like a teenager as he pulled into the Portsmouth parking garage. Strolling down Market Street, he smiled at the shop windows outlined with tiny white lights, or a mixture of blinking colored lights. The boutiques were filled with pretty gift boxes tied with glistening satin bows. Items shop owners had put on display to entice Christmas shoppers.

A Salvation Army bell ringer, bundled in a wool coat and muffler, was stationed by a lamppost. Georgie turned back dropping the coins in his pocket into her bucket."

"Thanks, and God bless you," she said with a warm smile.

Nodding, Georgie picked up his pace, eager to see Rosie.

Hustling to her door, he pressed the button for number 5. With a click releasing the door, he entered taking the steps two at a time to the second floor. Rosie was standing in the doorway to her studio apartment.

"Hi, come in, come in. You must be freezing," she said closing the door, with a slight toss of her head, flipping dark waves of inky black hair from her eyes.

"You look terrific, Rosie. It feels like years since I saw you," he said taking off his narrow brimmed black hat, a small feather tucked in the brim—his Sunday best.

"Not quite—a few weeks," she said offering him her cheek. "I'll get my coat. I like your hat," she said with a giggle, slipping on a cloche—black coat, black slacks. Her hat was adorned with a cluster of glossy beads in the folds of a satin bow. Two tiny feathers added a bit of whimsy.

"What?" she said, catching him looking at her.

"Nothing," he said, holding her coat. "You look more than terrific, Rosie. You're beautiful." He pulled her close, his lips seeking hers. He could feel her heart beating against his. He leaned back, looking into her jet black eyes. Yes, it was in the warmth of her eyes—she felt the same in his arms.

"What do you say we get some dinner, maybe a little dancing? Are you up for it?"

"Definitely, Mr. Wolfe, and I'm starving."

"Good. Me too. I know a little bar off Market Street. They feature new groups hoping to catch fire. Maybe you've been there," he said as she locked the door.

"Once, if it's the one I'm thinking of."

"Oh, oh. Want to go someplace else?"

She laughed. "It's a fun place, great music in the basement. I went there with a couple of nurses several months ago."

Georgie grasped her hand as they strode down Market Street. A few more blocks and they entered the old brick building, into the warmth of the cozy bar. The red brick walls and high ceiling of stained oak planking had been sand blasted removing years of grime, bringing the interior back to a lustrous life. Patrons were perched on a row of barstools chatting, laughing—carefree on a Saturday night. It was good to relax, out with friends, groups, or couples.

The hostess led them to a booth. Smiling, she laid down menus, ready to take their drink orders.

"What do you prefer, Rosie, on a cold night out on the town?"

"Umm, I think something that's warm all the way to my toes...a Manhattan, please."

"Make that two. Who's playing tonight downstairs?" he asked the waitress.

"A lovely group—oldies but goodies. Nine o'clock."

The drinks arrived, and the waitress took their dinner order—Rosie opted for fish and chips, Georgie a grilled steak.

Georgie tapped his glass to hers, "Cheers—to a wonderful evening."

"It already is," she said. "Have you heard from your dad? Is he enjoying Tel Aviv?"

"Not a word. It's only been two days. Finn said Danny called—checking on the farm I guess."

Their dinners, sizzling on hot plates, were set on the table. "My fish looks perfect. How's your steak?"

"Haven't tried yet, but the fries are perfect."

"Bradley Farm is beautiful. A wonderful place to grow up. And the farmhouse is like a Currier and Ives picture. I felt like I was stepping back in time," Rosie said.

"You should see it in the spring when the fields come to life, the sweet smell of the soil. Sometimes I slow down the tractor so I can feel the blades of the tiller slicing the earth, giving it air over the long winter packed down with snow."

"I can hear the birds singing in your picture. The passion you have for farming, the seedlings—much like mine with my patients. Many times they're struggling in a life or death situation when I see them in the ER," Rosie said. She looked away. Georgie laid his hand over hers, his thumb caressing her soft knuckles, coaching her back from a sad image.

"They don't all make it," she whispered.

"Hey, if you were the last one I saw, I would die happy." His voice was soft, comforting in whatever she was reliving. "How long have you been in the ER?"

"Hmm—six months."

"Rosie, how about spending Christmas at the farm with me? The family is away and—"

"Maybe another time. After tonight I'm working through Christmas. Mostly nights, some double shifts. I generally volunteer for holiday shifts—let those with families celebrate Christmas, especially if they have children."

The waitress stopped by the table. "Anything else I can get you two? The group is tuning up downstairs."

"Rosie, dessert?"

"I don't think so, maybe later."

"Well let's go check out the music." Georgie paid the check, picked up their coats and hats as Rosie shouldered her purse, and led the way to the stairs.

The female vocalist, crooning *Moon River*, beckoned them to come on down. A keyboard, fiddle, sax and percussion players completed the group, at times humming in the background or harmonizing with the singer as she caressed the microphone.

Georgie dropped their hats and coats on the chairs at a table for two. Leading Rosie to the dance floor, he gently pulled her into his arms.

At the group's break, they enjoyed another cocktail. Sharing small talk, laughing at the thought of Jeli playing tour guide, her arm looped through Gran's. After all, anyone who navigated the Great Wall of China could certainly find her way around Jerusalem. But as soon as the musicians struck the first cord, they were back on the dance floor.

Georgie didn't want the evening to end. Dancing, holding Rosie in his arms, he let his mind drift—what if? What if Rosie was with him always? Waking up in the morning with her snuggled against him? What if she was waiting for him as he hopped off the tractor at the end of a long day in the fields? What if she was dead on her feet? He'd massage her shoulders, her back, and her toes, ankles, after a tense operation in the OR.

Dancing to a ballad of love, he felt her arms reach up, fingers playing with his hair tied low at the nape of his neck.

"I should be going—double shift tomorrow. I don't want to, but—"

"Sure." He kissed her cheek, then slipped his hand in hers leading her to their coats, their hats.

Strolling to her apartment, bundled up against the chilly night, the shops were closed but the lights in the windows promised a busy day tomorrow. In the warm glow of being together, they spoke softly of the brilliance of the moon and stars.

He may say goodnight at her door, but it would not be for long. Georgie knew in his heart they would soon turn *what-ifs* into reality.

Chapter 26

———

THE AIR HAD TURNED BITTER cold. Another week would usher in a new year, the middle of winter but with the promise of spring to follow. Two men, nodding to each other, zipped up their leather jackets. Tonight was the night. Many phone calls, meetings, had taken place formulating the plans for the heist. All that was left was the opportunity. Staking out the farmhouse had been fruitless. They were frustrated, anxious to put the hours of planning into action, to strike.

But that changed when a few days ago the stakeout paid off. A large black van had pulled up to the farmhouse. The family members strolled out the back door. Suitcases were loaded into the van. Hugs, laughter, last minute instructions were given. The van drove off.

Voila!

A flurry of cell calls ensued. The family was obviously going on a trip. How long would they be gone? With the number of suitcases, it must be at least over Christmas.

———

CHRISTMAS DAY WAS WINDING down when Finn opened the brewpub at six o'clock. He promised some bikers and other townies they could drop by for a beer, leaving the stress of the holiday behind. Katie said she was fine with it, and arranged for Daisy to stay with Carrie until the pub closed.

At midnight, the groups of bikers in the brewpub dwindled down to three. Katie cleared the bottles, emptied the crumbs from the pretzel bowls as the bikers pushed back, stretched.

One walked over, squeezed her arm. "Thanks, Katie. Tell that husband of yours that the brewmaster's new specialty beer is a winner. See you next week."

"I'll be sure to tell Cam myself. You boys be safe. The roads are slippery out there."

Katie walked over to Finn who opened his arms pulling her onto his lap.

"So, are you and Georgie going to talk all night? Because if you are, I'm going to bed after I pick up Daisy."

"You go, babe. I'll be along in a few," Finn said.

Katie gave him a peck on the lips, grabbed her coat off a peg near the door, and slipped out letting the spring pull the door shut with a whoosh of frigid air.

Finn topped off his and Georgie's beer.

"How are you doing, Georgie? Still struggling with the idea there was some skullduggery with the barley?" Finn asked.

"Yep, I think there was foul play but I can't prove it. Only thing I know is that the last dumping didn't get wet enough to spoil the rest of the harvest. Larry made sure to dump the last cart on the floor away from the bins." Georgie shook his head. "I can't figure it out. The bins showed signs of moisture throughout, enough to cause mold. You tell me how that could happen—divine intervention to put you out of business?"

"I hear ya. In fact, I don't want to take any chances on another freak accident, or whatever it was that caused the barley to turn bad."

"What are you talking about?" George asked.

"Bullion's portrait and the gold bars. I say we go get both and take them to the house. Maybe Gran's bedroom. Somebody's in the house most of the day and little Scooter goes crazy if he hears a cricket. The family will be home in a few days. How about we go

move them to the house now? You and I can take turns sleeping—
"

"'I like the idea. But we both don't have to sleep on the couch in the farmhouse. Let's do it, but I'll stay tonight. You go home. Katie's waiting for you."

Putting their glasses in the dishwasher, Finn then turned off the lights. He locked up the pub, hustled to catch up with Georgie on the path to the horse barn.

"Shit," Georgie mumbled. "The barn door is open. I thought I closed it."

The pair strode into the barn, Georgie shaking his head. A streak of light slashed across the floor from Danny's workshop.

Turning the corner they saw two men wearing ski masks. Bullion's painting was on the floor, boards behind the painting thrown on top. The men were bent over, one with a bar in each hand, the other reaching for the third bar.

"Hey, drop those bars," Finn yelled charging forward.

Startled, the men snapped to attention. The one reaching for the third bar pulled a gun from his waist pointing it at Finn.

Georgie pushed Finn aside.

The gun fired.

Georgie went down falling across Finn.

The two robbers fled into the night as Finn squirmed out from under Georgie's lifeless body, his blood leaking from under his jacket.

Katie rushed in, Cam and Carrie behind her.

"Finn, I heard a gunshot. What are you two—" Katie started to say.

"Call 9-1-1," Finn shouted. "Hurry. Georgie's been shot."

Chapter 27

———

CAMERON STOOD WAVING FRANTICALLY at the ambulance racing up the driveway. The red light on the roof whirled sending blood-red beams of light pulsating over the fields, punctuating the inky night air. The ambulance driver followed Cameron down the dirt path, pulling to a stop at the gaping entrance to the horse barn. He jumped out from behind the wheel, as the medic in the passenger seat scrambled to remove a stretcher.

The two medics entered the horse barn, the woodworking shop, moving in front of Finn to tend to the victim. Finn let go of the jacket he used to apply pressure to Georgie's wound, trying to contain the flow of blood.

In short order, the medics anchored Georgie to the stretcher, hustling him into the van. Finn jumped in as the door shut. The driver backed up the dirt path. Navigating a three-point turn by the house, they sped down the driveway. When the van turned east out of the driveway, a squad car turned in.

Inside the van the medic cut away Georgie's clothing exposing the wound to his belly. He kept adding dressings, pressing on the gauze, trying to stem the bleeding—unsuccessfully. The driver called the Portsmouth Level II Trauma Center, alerting the emergency staff they were on the way with a gunshot victim, unconscious but alive.

Finn sat beside Georgie holding onto his leg. The medic, applying pressure with one hand, checked Georgie's vitals with the other. He turned to Finn. "What's your name? A relative?"

Finn hesitated. "Finn Bradley. Georgie lives with us on the farm."

———

AT 2:05 A.M. THE DOCTOR checked Georgie's condition, and immediately ordered he be taken to the OR. The hall outside the OR was brilliant-white cement block, the fluorescent lights belying the fact that a man lay near death in the next room. Finn sat on a hard bench, hands behind his neck, looking to the ceiling.

"Please, dear God, don't let Georgie die," Finn whispered. "I love him like a brother, he saved—"

"Mr. Bradley?" The nurse in blue scrubs touched his arm.

"Yes, Finn Bradley. Has—"

"Mr. Wolfe needs blood."

Finn jumped to his feet. Mr. Wolfe? "Oh, yes…Mr. Wolfe. Take mine, my blood."

"I doubt you have his blood type, but—"

"I don't know my blood type, but let's check."

"Come with me," the nurse said.

"Why do you say you doubt I'm a match?" Finn asked matching the nurse stride for stride.

"In here, sir. Take off your shirt. Here's a Johnny…it's chilly in here. By the way, your wife called. She'll be here soon with a change of clothes. Yours…well, they're very bloody."

"Okay, sure, but what blood type is Georgie?"

"It's very rare—AB Negative. Does Mr. Wolfe have any family—"

"Yes, his dad, but he's in Israel. He and my family are visiting my brother. But wait, they're due to land in Boston tomorrow."

"What time, Mr. Bradley?"

"Ah, around noon, I think."

"That will be too late. The hospital has put out an emergency request for several pints, but so far none of the blood banks have the type the patient needs. As I said, it's very rare."

Finn removed his shirt, hesitated. He didn't realize Georgie's blood soaked his clothes. He sat down, held out his arm, palm up.

The nurse swabbed his arm inside his elbow, inserted the needle withdrawing a small vial of blood. "Mr. Bradley, do you want to donate a pint for the blood bank? Actually with your size, you could give two pints. In the event we find a match for Mr. Wolfe's blood, yours will offset the cost of the blood we receive."

"Sure, sure, okay. Now?"

"I'll just take this sample to the lab. I'll be right back. Have you given blood before?"

"No, as I said, I don't know my type."

"Right. I'll let you know when your wife arrives. What's her name?" the nurse asked.

"Katie, Katie Bradley." Finn sat back in the cold vinyl chair. How could this be happening?

He reached in his pants pocket to retrieve his phone. The cover was bloody. Georgie's blood.

Finn scrolled to Sadie's number. She would be in the air, but at least he could leave a message. He closed the cell. What message should he leave? He decided to say the truth, just not the whole truth.

"Hi, sis. Call me as soon as you land in Boston. There's been an accident. Georgie's in the hospital. He was shot. I'm with him—the Portsmouth Regional Hospital. Call me. Love you."

Bursting through the door, the nurse looked at Finn, a wide smile on her face. "Now, Mr. Bradley, please lay down on the table. A nurse is on her way with the kit to take your blood. I have to ask you a few questions, then we'll go ahead."

"So, what type am I?"

"AB Negative. Mr. Wolfe is an incredibly lucky man to have you as a friend."

Chapter 28

THE OPERATION WAS OVER. The doctor had done all he could. It was now up to the man lying on the operating table. Did he have the will to live, or would he succumb to his wounds?

Backing away from his patient, the doctor nodded to the OR nurse. She nodded in return. She knew what to do.

Orderlies were summoned, carefully wheeling the man on the table to the recovery room. The nurse followed the orderlies. It would be awhile before the sedation wore off, awhile before they would know if he was going to survive the trauma to his body.

The nurse quickly checked that the probes were still in place, that the monitors were updating the information—heart rate, blood pressure, vital signs. Two hours later the doctor approved his transfer to the Critical Care Unit. Once Georgie was settled, the orderlies turned to leave the ICU, the last one addressing the nurse. "Let us know if there's anything more we can do, Rosie."

"I will, thanks. There is one more thing. Please tell his friend, Finn Bradley, that he can come see Mr. Wolfe. He's waiting in a room down the hall."

Rosie looked down at Georgie. He was pale, vulnerable. She touched his arm. It was cold. She laid another blanket over him, tucking it close to his body.

The lights were dimmed, the cool air filled with an antiseptic scent. The day was a blur—two transfusions, hours in the operating room. But he was still alive and Rosie knew she would stay the night by his side.

Hearing footsteps at the door, Rosie glanced up. It was Finn.

"Rosie? Oh my God, I didn't know you were a nurse here. Georgie...Georgie stepped in front of me, he took the bullet...Rosie, he saved my life." Finn was trying to retain his composure, his heart beating so fast it felt like it would pop out of his chest. "He looks awful." Finn touched the blanket. "Is he going to be okay?"

"I pray so," Rosie said. "What happened, Finn?" she whispered trying to guide him to a chair, but he wouldn't budge from Georgie's side.

"It was late. We were talking in the pub. The last of the bikers left." Finn tried to catch his breath. Almost panting as he explained to Rosie what happened. "We had this idea that we should move Bullion's painting and the gold bars to the house, to Gran's room. We thought they would be safer. Someone's almost always in the house. When we got to the barn...Rosie, two masked men had uncovered the bars. They were stealing them. I yelled at them to get out."

Finn paused, chocking up, fingers gently touching the blanket covering Georgie's shoulder.

"What happened next, Finn? The surgeon removed a bullet—how..."

"One of the men pulled a gun. It happened so fast...Georgie pushed me away, the gun went off, Georgie fell on top of me. The men—they ran out. Seconds later, Katie ran in. I yelled at her to call 911. Rosie, he's going to be okay—right?"

Rosie shook her head. "You know him. Is he a fighter?"

"Oh, uh. Well, I think so."

"What do you mean—you think so?"

"Lately he's been...I don't know...hard to describe. Questioning stuff about his life. Rosie, I'm glad you're here. He never brought anyone home for dinner before."

Finn staggered reaching for the end of the bed to steady himself.

Rosie grabbed a chair and pulled it to the side of the bed. "Sit down, Finn. You just gave a lot of blood. I shouldn't have let you stand."

"Thanks, I'll be okay. You know I had the same blood type?"

"Yes, the nurse told me. A miracle. Here, drink this water. I'll get some orange juice for you. You need fluids. I'm shocked you guys had the same blood type. George saved your life and you saved his."

Rosie saw Georgie's finger move. Her eyes darted to the monitor checking his heartbeat. It was weak but regular. His eyelashes fluttered, he looked at her for an instant then his eyes closed. Rosie fished her fingers under the blanket, squeezed his hand. She was sure she felt him squeeze back, not much but a little. Her eyes welled up, but she quickly turned away from Finn, pretending to tuck her hair in back of her ear as she swiped a tear from her eye.

———

SADIE AND TRAVIS HAD tickets to fly home to Washington D.C. leaving Wolfe in charge to rent a car, driving Gran, Jane and Danny to the farm. Jeli wasn't able to get a ticket on the same flight. She was booked on the next one connecting in Paris to Boston. All that changed when Sadie checked her cell as she stood in line to deplane in Boston. She listened to Finn's message. After a quick conversation with him, they decided to rent an SUV.

Travis drove the car north on I-95 to Portsmouth.

Around one in the afternoon, the family arrived at the hospital. They all trooped from the parking lot into the ER waiting room. Sadie identified herself as George Wolfe's family and asked to speak to a doctor about his condition. Where was he now? Where was her brother Finn Bradley?

The guard behind the window asked for identification. She nudged Wolfe to show his driver's license with his name, verifying he was Georgie's father. The guard asked them to have a seat, saying a nurse would be out shortly to meet with them.

"Great, but, sir, we want to *see* George Wolfe and my brother Finn."

"I know. Please have a seat."

Gran and Danny sat down, he rubbing his knee. Rushing was never good, but he didn't complain. The others stood. Travis leaned against the wall as Sadie paced. Wolfe remained outside on the sidewalk, the collar on his coat turned up around his ears.

The door opened to the right of the guard's window and Rosie stepped into the cramped emergency check-in area.

"Rosie, you're a nurse here?" Sadie said.

"Yes. George is critical, but his condition has been stable since the operation."

One by one, Rosie received their hugs. They stood in a semi-circle in front of her. "He needs more blood." She looked from one to the other, concern written on her face.

Danny stood up. "I'll go talk to Wolfe," Danny said. Finn and Rosie stepped outside with him.

Wolfe continued pacing outside the emergency entrance. Danny put his arm around Wolfe's shoulders, around the man who helped him beat his depression, helped him beat the worthlessness he felt coming home from the war missing a leg.

"Wolfe, your son needs your help," Danny said. "Finn has already given two pints so he can't donate more now."

"I can't," Wolfe replied turning away.

Chapter 29

WOLFE'S BREATHING WAS LABORED as he looked over the parking lot. The siren of an ambulance screamed in the distance.

Finn and Rosie looked from Wolfe to Danny. *How could a father not help save his son?*

Danny shook Wolfe's arm. "Why not, for god's sake?"

"Mr. Wolfe, please come with me? There's a good chance you have the same rare blood type," Rosie said

Wolfe stepped back, confused, stammered. "Oh, no, I…"

"It's okay, Mr. Wolfe, it won't take long. I'll stay with you, but we should go now," Rosie said turning to the door. Wolfe didn't move.

"I…I'm afraid of hospitals. I can't do this. Kids where I grew up went to the hospital and never came back. If I go in, Georgie won't come back."

"I don't know what happened back then, but this is a standard procedure. Georgie needs you," Finn said. He stood nose to nose, fists balled ready to jab the man's chest. This was not the man he grew up with, like a member of the family. The homeless man carrying a baby in a basket that Gran had taken under her wing, paid to renovate the tree house so he and his son would have a home.

"Maybe our bloods don't match up." Wolfe muttered.

"Even if they don't, your blood can be banked for a pint that Georgie needs," Danny said. "We're going to give, all of us. Jeli too. She's on her way," Danny said. "Come on, we'll do it together."

Wolfe, face contorted, tears welling, turned, looked into Danny's eyes.

Was Wolfe going to run away? Run from what?

"I'll go with you," he whispered.

Finn let out a breath of air. He wasn't sure what just happened, but Wolfe agreeing to donate blood had to be good for Georgie.

Rosie led the men inside. The women were filling out forms on clipboards.

The nurse gathering the information looked at Wolfe, raised her brows. Wolfe nodded. She handed him a clipboard, another to Danny. Travis handed his form to the nurse. "Ladies, come along, we'll take your blood first, then the men's."

Sadie handed the nurse her clipboard, and turned to Rosie. "I have a twin brother in Israel. Given Finn was a match, should we ask for his blood type? And regardless, can he give blood there?"

"Yes, find out his blood type. If by any chance his is the same, and if George needs more…but, I'm afraid it won't be in time."

Just as the family thought there might be hope, Rosie's words socked them in the belly. Surely there was hope Georgie was going to recover. Surely?

"When can we see him?" Sadie asked.

"He's in ICU, still sedated. You can look in on him after you give blood."

Suddenly the outside door flew open. Jeli breezed in. "How is he?"

"Not good, Jeli-bean," Finn said.

"We're giving blood," Sadie said. "Can you come with us? Gran is sitting this one out."

"Of course," Jeli said nodding, her eyes darting around at the blank faces.

Jeli touched Katie's arm. "How's Daisy? When I called you from the airport for more info, Carrie answered. She said you were at the hospital. Anyway, I heard Daisy crying."

"She's very upset but calmed down a little. I didn't want her to see Georgie so I left her with Carrie and Cam.

———

THE FAMILY LOOKED IN on Georgie through the window of the ICU. No one said anything, their faces grim. Georgie was hooked up to monitors, necessary fluids and a drip-bag delivering medications. Rosie was swapping an empty drip bag with a fresh one. She smiled tentatively to the family on the other side of the window.

Sadie stepped back. "Let's go to the cafeteria, get some coffee and talk about what to do."

Katie led the way, she had been to the cafeteria earlier, also spent time in the chapel praying for Georgie's recovery.

Travis pulled two tables up so they could all sit together.

"Mom, I think you and Pops and Gran should go home," Sadie said. "Travis and I will go with you...we'll stay overnight. Hopefully, Georgie will start coming out of it in the morning, at least we'll have more information. Nothing more we can do here now."

"Yes, that's a good idea," Jane said, patting Gran's hand.

"I'm staying with Georgie," Finn said. He glanced at Wolfe. "How about you, Wolfe?"

"Me? I..."

"Come with us, Wolfe," Danny said sending a sharp glance at Finn.

"Hey, there everyone. The nurse said I'd find you here." Sheriff Townsend said approaching the family.

Finn jumped to his feet. "Tommy, any news on the two guys? Who they are?"

"Afraid not, Finn. We don't have much to go on. One important question for you. You said there were three gold bars. The perps left with two. I wanted to let you know that I bagged the third bar and the painting after you left with the medics. The lab is dusting the painting for fingerprints and taking pictures of the gold bar. The pics have been sent out alerting all departments in New England to be on the lookout for anyone trying to sell them. There are distinguishing marks from the mold used to caste the gold. It won't be easy for them to sell the bars, so that's in our favor. If nothing turns up by tonight we'll expand the alert across the country. While I have you here, I'd like you to tell me who knew about the gold."

"All of us here," Finn said, glancing around the table. "We were the only ones...except for Cam and Carrie. They know. I told them."

"And our little girl, Daisy," Katie said. "She's home with the Fosters. She loves Georgie and in a little girl's eyes, she's sure he is going die. She's very upset."

"We were all in the barn after we found the gold, then we went down to the pub to celebrate. As you know, Tommy, things haven't been going well...the barley rotting. Which, as you also know, Georgie thinks was sabotage. Sabotage or not, we were facing bankruptcy.

"Any sign there's a connection, Sheriff?" Travis said.

All eyes turned to Travis. Did the FBI agent know something? What were they missing?

Chapter 30

IT WAS LATE AFTERNOON and the sun hit Travis in the eyes as he drove the family to the farm. Parking the car near the back door, he and Wolfe hauled the suitcases to the various bedrooms. Katie hurried down the path to the lake, to the two tiny houses located a few yards apart—Finn and Katie's, and the Foster's.

Carrie turned from the window. "Your mommy's here, Daisy," she said.

The little girl squirted around Carrie, running outside. Katie scooped Daisy into her arms. Her beautiful little girl with red eyes swollen from crying, clung to her mommy, but the tears had stopped.

"Is Uncle Georgie dead?" Daisy asked, snuggling against Katie kneeling on the frosted leaves, cradling her daughter.

"No, sweetheart, Uncle Georgie is in the hospital. He's very sick, but…" she left the word hanging. Katie couldn't say he would be okay because he was still fighting for his life. "Let's go up to the big house. Everyone is asking about you. They all love you, Daisy."

Katie set Daisy on her feet and thanked Carrie and Cam who were standing in their doorway.

Cam mouthed, "How is he really?"

"Not good," Katie mouthed back shaking her head.

"Does he still need blood?" Carrie asked.

"Yes. He has a rare type. We've all given to the blood bank. Miraculously, Finn matched Georgie's. I don't know what type everyone else is. I do know mine wasn't a match."

JANE STOOD AT THE SINK, looking out the window. It was a gloomy day. Sleeting now and then portending a snowstorm wasn't far off.

"Tommy just turned up our driveway in his sheriff's car. Must be official," she said.

"I'll get the door," Danny said, grabbing his cane.

Tommy popped the trunk of his squad car, lifted out Bullion's painting wrapped in plastic and a box wrapped in brown paper.

"Travis, can you help us out here?" Danny called.

"On my way," Travis replied pulling his arms through the sleeves of his coat.

"Here, Travis, you take the painting, and Danny this is for you—the gold bar," Tommy said.

The three men walked into the kitchen, Tommy following behind Danny.

"Cup of coffee, Tommy, and—" Jane stopped short seeing the painting Travis was holding as he removed the plastic.

"Returning your property, Jane," Tommy said.

Danny laid the package wrapped in brown paper on the kitchen table. "And, here's the gold bar. Question is, where to put these for safe keeping?"

"That's easy," Travis said. "The cellar, the Underground Railroad cavern that Georgie uncovered."

"Perfect and fitting. Georgie's still on the job," Danny said with a chuckle. Travis, you and Tommy do the honors before our sheriff leaves today."

Katie was holding Daisy on her lap. She turned her face away, closed her eyes, and began sobbing again.

"Hey, baby girl, what's wrong?" Katie said.

Jeli, sitting next to Katie, patted the little girl's back, comforting her.

"Mommy, I'm sorry," Daisy said gulping for air. Danny handed his big-grandpa handkerchief from his pocket to Katie. She mopped away Daisy's tears, but they kept streaming down her cheeks.

"What are you sorry about, sweetie?" Katie said.

"It's all my fault, Mommy. Will I be struck by lightning, like the movie I saw last night?"

"Heavens no. I don't know what you saw, but come on I'll take you home—"

"No. No. We have to pray for Uncle Georgie. That's what the woman in the movie did. It's my fault Uncle Georgie's dying."

"He's not dying," Gran said. "But tell us why you think this is your fault? I'm sure there is no way you can be responsible."

"At the celebration in Daddy's pub, I told the man about a pot of gold and that it's guarded by a golden horse."

Eyes popped. Jaws dropped.

Gran started to say something but it was garbled.

"What did you say, Gran?" Jelli asked.

"Sorry, my tongue got in front of my eyetooth and I couldn't see," she laughed. "My mother's favorite saying."

"What's that supposed to mean, Gran?" Danny asked.

"I see that Daisy is a smart little girl who just put a big piece in the puzzle."

Jeli gently turned Daisy so they could look eye to eye.

"Daisy, exactly when and how many men did you talk to at the pub?" Jeli asked gently patting the little girl's arm.

"Thanksgiving. I was putting pretzels in the bowl."

"This was after we were in the horse barn and Finn and Georgie removed the piece of wood revealing the yellow bricks?"

Daisy nodded.

"And the men were sitting at a table in your daddy's pub?"

"Yes. There were lots of people. I was very busy. When I added pretzels to their bowl, they said I looked very happy and that my daddy looked very happy too. They asked me why we were happy. They were laughing. I laughed too, and said it was because we found a pot of gold."

Daisy began to cry again, "Grandpops told us in the barn not to tell anyone about the gold. I didn't mean to, it just came out."

"It's okay, Daisy. I love you, and you're very brave to tell us your secret," Jane said. "Secrets are meant to be kept secret, but sometimes we do things and we want to tell someone, like our family because they love us, and can help us. And that's what you did, baby girl. You knew you had to tell your secret because it might mean helping to find the men who made Uncle Georgie sick."

Jeli jumped out of her seat. "Wait here everyone, especially you, Daisy," she called over her shoulder as she charged up the two flights of stairs to her bedroom, then came thumping back down to the kitchen. She had her phone in her hand. Her fingers gingerly swiping the glass display several times then stopped. She leaned into Daisy so the little girl could see the phone.

"Daisy, I took these pictures that night. Remember, I showed up after dinner and after you found the gold. Now look hard, tell me if you see the two men."

Tommy and Travis walked behind Katie and watched as Jeli slowly swiped one picture to the next.

"You were busy as you said, Daisy. You're in several of these pics. Do you see the men?" Jeli asked.

Daisy shook her head.

"How about this one? Two men and you. Look, you twirled I think and—"

Daisy's finger shot out, touching the phone.

"These two are the men you told about the pot of gold?" Jeli asked, passing her phone so everyone could see.

"Yes, I'm sorry, Aunt Jeli."

"Nothing to be sorry about, Daisy. I dub you *Miss Private Investigator*," Tommy said patting Daisy's shoulder. "Good work, Miss Investigator. Jeli, please send me those pictures, and any others—heck, send them all. Here's my cell number," Tommy said handing her his business card. "Anyone recognize these guys?" Tommy asked.

"No idea," Pops said. Tommy looked from one to the other. All shook their heads.

Chapter 31

———

LAKEVILLE'S POLICE DEPARTMENT was a small outpost tied to the Portsmouth PD. Small was an understatement. It consisted of Sheriff Tommy Townsend, a high school football hero. He and Finn were on the team together. Townsend had a deputy, Gomer Tipton, and an office manager. Lakeville PD also had a small lab manned by a tech who dropped in once a week from Portsmouth PD.

Tommy was anxious to see how Georgie was doing. He also wanted to talk to Finn again about the robbery. He checked in at the ICU nurse's station and was told that Mr. Wolfe was alert, talking. He was gaining strength after the blood transfusions.

"What about the blood situation? Need any more?" Townsend asked.

The nurse checked her computer before answering. "As I said, he seems stable. You'd have to talk to the doctor. His friend is with him. Maybe he'll have more information."

Townsend let out a puff of air. He wasn't a member of the family, and he didn't say he was on official business.

Strolling down the brilliant lighting in the hall, he pulled out a pad of paper checking the list of questions he wanted to ask Finn. Looking in the window at Georgie, Rosie was holding a straw to his lips with ice water. Finn was sitting in a chair beside his bed—a welcome sight. Townsend rapped softly on the window.

Finn patted Georgie's hand and stepped out into the hall.

"Tommy, any leads?"

"Can we go down to the cafeteria?"

"Sure, I could use a cup of coffee."

Sitting at a table with their coffees, Tommy pulled out his phone. "You asked about a lead. We may have one and from a source you won't believe."

"Who?" Finn asked.

"Daisy. She said something about a pot of gold guarded by a golden horse when pouring pretzels in a bowl for two men at the pub. This was after you found the gold bars. They asked why she and her daddy were so happy."

"Maybe that's why she's been crying?" Finn said.

"Seems so. How's that for a huge stroke of luck? She felt she was to blame for Georgie being shot. She kept asking if he was dead. Now, get this. Jeli took pictures around the pub that night. I guess she arrived late?"

"Yes, she did. She was in China, a furniture deal. Surprising us, she came straight from the airport. Come on, Tommy. Are you saying Jeli has a pic?"

"We can't be sure, and you didn't get a look at their faces because they were wearing ski masks."

"Show me. Show me. Maybe I know them. I was scared. Maybe I missed something."

Tommy pulled up the picture of Daisy talking to the two men laughing.

Finn's shoulders slumped. "I don't know them. Worse, I can't say I've ever seen them in the pub."

"Well, I've sent a copy to my deputy, Gomer Tipton, to keep his eyes out around town—drugstore, grocery store, café—maybe he'll spot them. It's getting cold out, maybe they'll be stupid enough to put on those ski masks," Tommy said with a chuckle.

"If they stole the bars, I'm guessing they're long gone," Finn said.

"Maybe yes, maybe no. We'll see. Did Georgie tell you about Cameron's insurance policy?"

"Yep, but I didn't ask Cam about it. Figured it was his business. I couldn't bring myself to question him. Hey, can I hitch a ride back to Lakeville with you?"

"Sure, I'll take you back to the farm. Let's talk to Cam if he's around."

"Do I have to?"

"Just working the case, Finn. From all angles."

"Got it. Poor Daisy. Rosie said Georgie may be moved out of the ICU tonight. Give me a minute to let Rosie know I'm leaving. If they do move Georgie, I'll see if I can bring Daisy to see him, see that he's alive."

"Good idea," Tommy said.

Finn stopped to let Georgie know he was heading to the farm and that he'd be back tomorrow. Rosie followed him out to the hall.

"Finn, thanks for staying with George. You're a good friend."

"I think you being by his side is way more important to our friend than I am. You should go home, get some sleep yourself. He's not going anywhere," Finn said, chuckling.

Finn hustled out of the hospital, slid into the squad car's passenger seat. "How do you want to handle the conversation with Cameron?" he asked, glancing at Tommy.

"Keep yourself in his corner. We don't want him to think we're ganging up on him. You know?" Tommy said.

"Sure. What about Carrie? Do we talk to Cam alone or with her?"

"Definitely alone. She may not know about the policy, or maybe she does. The little I've talked to Cam, he seems to be the boss in the family."

"They're good people, Tommy. He's my partner. He knows everything about me—"

"But I'm thinking you don't know everything about him."

As the sun set, the squad car turned up the driveway to Bradley Farm. There were several cars parked at the pub, double that with motorcycles.

"Let's go in the pub. Cam's probably tending bar. If Carrie's there, I can ask her to take over a few minutes while we bring Cam up-to-date about Georgie," Finn said.

"Sounds right," Tommy said.

The pair strolled into the pub, Tommy taking a seat off to the side near the bar. As Finn had planned he asked Carrie to tend bar for a few minutes so he and Cam could talk to the sheriff about the harvest and what Georgie thought was sabotage.

Finn filled two glasses with beer from the tap, light on foam, for Cam and Tommy. Cam, a trim black man, followed him to the table but declined the beer as did Tommy, shaking his head as Finn approached.

"Have it your way, Tommy, as for me a frosty beer, this is one of Cam's specialties, it is going to taste mighty sweet after the last two days."

"Cameron, you know I've been talking to everyone on the farm about the night of the harvest. All routine, learning about everyone's situation that night," Townsend said.

"I don't understand what you mean by *learning* everyone's situation," Cam said.

"Just that—all routine. Financial stuff, Finn's finances. Would he be in hock, bad financial situation where he could improve, handle his debts by declaring bankruptcy? Take you, you have an insurance policy on the business in case of bankruptcy."

"Snooping around in my personal affairs, Sheriff? Finn, I thought you asked me to have a beer with Sheriff Townsend, an update. Now you're accusing me of sabotaging our business?" Cam's voice rose as he got to his feet. "Well, I resent the implication, ask me straight out or charge me, but don't play games."

Cam stomped off, shoved passed Carrie behind the bar, disappearing into the brewery, the doors swinging shut behind him.

―――

CARRIE SLIPPED INTO THE brewery leaving Finn in stunned silence at his partner's words.

"What's the matter with you, Cam? I heard the sheriff. You didn't tell me about any bankruptcy insurance," Carrie said.

Cam faced her. "It's routine. There's nothing to know," Cameron snapped, banging out the back door, stalking up the path.

Carrie was on his heels, grabbed his arm.

He shrugged her off.

They crested the hill, marched down to the edge of the lake, passing their tiny house. It was freezing out but neither seemed to notice.

"Talk to me, Cam," Carrie shouted stepping in front of him, fire in her eyes.

"Maybe this deal isn't right for us," Cam retorted.

"Give me a little more information, Mr. Foster. What isn't right—a brewery you've always dreamed of? That isn't right?"

"It's not ours, Carrie, in case you haven't notice. It's on Bradley Farm. My partner is a Bradley. And then there's the little situation of rotting grain bringing us to the brink of bankruptcy—"

"Bankruptcy isn't going to happen. The Bradleys are going to invest in the future of the brewpub, in case you haven't heard—plowing in the crazy gold they inherited. They're sharing—"

"I don't want sharing. There are more opportunities out there. Better ones."

"Where is *out there*, Cam? You were a hired hand at a tiny-house construction company. You were tinkering with home brewing in a shed until Finn came along, offering you a partnership. Bringing your dream of brewing your own craft beer to reality, a partnership—Finn out front with the customers, the Bradleys with farmland, and Georgie willing to grow hops and barley. And you have the gall to tell me there are more opportunities out there? Opportunities you won't say who with, or where?"

"Close by. That's all I can say."

"You wrench me from parents in Colorado, haul our little home to the other end of the earth, and now, now that I love it in Lakeville, you're saying give it up, *honey*?" Carrie snapped.

"It's Georgie's fault the grain is rotting—what kind of a farmer let's that happen. It's Finn's fault for spending too much money on the pub, and, and, I can't do anything about it. I want my own brewery—no partners."

"Well, don't count on me following."

Carrie stormed off, slamming the door of their house in his face.

Chapter 32

———

NIGHT FELL, ACTIVITY SLOWED in the halls of the hospital. Visitors had left, carts with empty meal trays rolled back to the kitchen.

It was Georgie's second night out of the ICU. Sadie and Travis dropped by earlier in the day on their way to the airport, returning home to Washington D.C. Jeli drove Gran, Pops, and Jane to the hospital for a brief visit, followed by Katie and Finn. They brought Daisy who stood on a small stool by Georgie's bed. Laying her head on his chest, arms around his neck, a fresh burst of tears rolled down her cheeks. This time they were happy tears. Uncle Georgie was alive.

Wolfe didn't join the family at the hospital. He said he'd wait, bring Georgie home when he was ready to come back to the farm.

Rosie dimmed the light in Georgie's room. She sat in the chair vacated when the last of the Bradleys sauntered out.

"You're doing so well, Mr. Wolfe," Rosie said smiling, slipping her hand under his. You're going home tomorrow. Of course, you unmercifully badgered the doctor to release you. He told you only on one condition could you go home—you have to take it easy, especially the first few days. Promise me you'll follow his orders?"

"I promise." Georgie squeezed her delicate fingers, a strong *I'm ready to go home* kind of squeeze.

"When I was first brought to the hospital, the operating room, were you there or was I dreaming?"

"You weren't dreaming. I was there. Your wound was so bad...lost so much blood, I was frightened that you weren't going to make it through the operation. I didn't realize how strong you were—body and spirit." She raised his hand to her cheek.

"Fooled you?"

"Yes, you did. I'm surprised you thought it was me—a surgical mask, scrubs, I hardly—"

"Your eyes. The first thing I noticed in the coffee shop was your eyes—sad that day, but in the brilliant light of the OR, your eyes were warm, caring."

"My, my, that's a lot considering you were unconscious when they wheeled you in." Rosie leaned close, softly placing her lips on his.

"What are your dreams, Rosie? A dream where you picture yourself, a picture you want to step into?"

"Oh, that's easy. I saw a movie once where lovers were dancing at the Ritz in Boston, the ballroom. The scene was powerful. I wanted to be that woman."

"Hmm, the Ritz," Georgie said, his voice hushed as his finger traced her cheek, her lips. "Tell me what you see."

Rosie laid her head on Georgie's arm, their fingers intertwined.

"The ballroom is enormous, ringed with delicate gold chairs, small round tables. Centered on each table is a crystal vase of white lilies set on a deep purple tablecloth. Fine white china. Cut crystal goblets are filled with bubbling champagne. There are slivers of decadent chocolate cake slathered with creamy fudge icing. The walls are covered with rich gold and purple silk. The floor to ceiling windows look out onto the Boston Commons, the trees aglow with tiny white lights sprinkled over the branches."

"And what is the beautiful lady wearing?"

"Ah, a creamy white flapper dress edged with gold beaded fringe. Every time the man twirls me under his arm, the fringe flares out. The dress is encrusted with swirls of gold sequins and has a scoop neck—front and back, showing lots of skin. I'm wearing gloves that match the dress, from my elbows to my fingertips. My shiny black hair is curved around my chin. A thin silk band of sequins is around my forehead."

Rosie sighed, eyes closed, seeing herself in the ballroom.

"My lover—tall, dark, and handsome of course—"

"Of course," Georgie whispered, his eyes grazing her face, her face glowing as she danced in the ballroom.

"He is strong guiding me over the gleaming dance floor. His black suit impeccable, the white shirt open just enough to show a tuft of black chest hair—so sexy I melt into his arms. We embrace and dance again. A full orchestra is playing—we are the only ones in the room. The scent of the lilies is heady and…"

Rosie lifted her head, smiled. "That is my dream, to dance at the Ritz," she said with a giggle.

"When I'm healed, Rosie, I'll take you dancing at the Ritz. I want to be the man escorting you on his arm in your dream."

Rosie lowered her lips to his ear. "You *are* the man in my dreams," she whispered.

Georgie turned his head accepting her kiss.

"When we first met at the coffee house—" Rosie started to say.

"I believe with all my heart, that events led me to Portsmouth that day, that time, that place. The only empty chair was at the table where you were sitting. Rosie, I think it was our destiny to meet. I love you, Rosie Castine, from Castine, Maine. Do you think you could ever love a farmer?"

"Hmm, that's a pretty big question, Mr. Wolfe."

"Well?"

"That depends on the farmer, but I have to say you look exactly like the tall, dark, handsome man in my dream. If he is the farmer you're asking about, then in answer to your question, I love that farmer more than he'll ever know. The land, a farm is the bedrock of a family…that kind of love, Mr. Wolfe. I grew up an orphan. To love a man who happens to be a farmer fills my heart beyond my dreams."

With some difficulty and some support from Rosie, Georgie sat up in bed, gingerly dangling his legs over the edge of the bed. He was eager to get back to his life. A life with Rosie?

Chapter 33

———

EARLY AFTERNOON, THE HOSPITAL halls were absent of the usual hustle and bustle of the lunchtime clatter—rolling carts hauling empty trays back to the kitchen. It was too early for the rush of visitors.

Wolfe sauntered into the hospital. He stopped at the nurse's station asking if George Wolfe was ready to be discharged. He was there to take Georgie home. The nurse checked her computer. Without looking up, she said, "Yes, but there's a note here that the doctor wants to see you. If you'll have a seat in the waiting area, I'll let the doctor know you're here. It won't be but a moment."

Looking down the hall to Georgie's room, Wolfe sighed, turned in the opposite direction, and walked to take a seat in the open area where he had waited for word on Georgie's condition several days ago.

The doctor whisked down the hall, stethoscope swinging over his green scrubs. Approaching, he stuck out his hand to Wolfe. "Let's take a walk, Mr. Wolfe, I'd like a private word with you."

Wolfe obliged following the doctor to an alcove by the elevators. The doctor stopped, turned to Wolfe.

"Mr. Wolfe, as you know your blood type did not match George's. We don't know what type his mother had but we can guess she was a match. There are blood subtypes determined by the presence, or absence, of antigens which can trigger a patient's immune system to attack transfused blood. That's why blood matching is critical. Finn Bradley's blood had some of these antigens, which is why George gained strength so rapidly. I was intrigued by what I found in the various blood types of those who made donations to the blood bank on George's behalf. I looked further to other markers that might disprove a theory I had developed. I found nothing. Bottom line, Mr. Wolfe, the probability of your being his father is zero."

Wolfe's face drained of all color. He fell back against the wall, staring into the doctor's eyes. He took several deep breaths. His breathing eased from the spike when the doctor said there was zero chance he was Georgie's father. Color returned. "You're right. I'm not Georgie's father. There are reasons—"

"Mr. Wolfe, I'm not telling you this to judge you. Your relationship with George is personal. However, I've learned that such a secret, in most cases, is better if you let it go, better to divulge the secret before it is discovered in an adversarial way. If you would like me to tell George, with or without your presence, I would be glad to help. If not, I will not divulge what I've found to George. What would you like me to do?"

"I'll take care of it, doctor. Now, please excuse me. I'm going to take Georgie home."

Wolfe turned away from the doctor and strode to Georgie's room. Rosie had helped him into a wheelchair, a pair of crutches lying across the arms of the chair. Rosie held a small case in her hand.

"Hello, Mr. Wolfe. George is ready for the trip. I'm going to follow in my car. I have a supply of dressings, ointment, and other incidentals I think you, or Jane, will need to change his dressing. He's healing nicely but I think you'll find them helpful," she said smiling. "He still struggles to stand up—stitches pulling. But once he's home, he should be able to stand up straight in a couple of days after the stitches are removed."

Wolfe glanced around the room. "That's it then. Rosie, if you can you handle the wheelchair, I'll bring the car around to the entrance."

Chapter 34

NEW YEARS EVE, New Years Day came and went. The brewpub revelers watched one football game after the other before and after toasting the new year.

Until Georgie could walk standing up straight without crutches, Jane and Gran insisted he stay in the guest room on the first floor of the big house. Jane could tend to his wound, and he could have his meals with the family without trudging back and forth on an icy path.

They enjoyed his company, especially Gran. They had long chats about Jane's plans for the gift and antique shops. They listened to his plans for the spring crop of barley and hops and how he could lay out the herb garden and a pumpkin patch for families in the fall.

Georgie had been home three days and was feeling pretty chipper, especially after phone conversations with Rosie. He hadn't seen her since the day he was discharged from the hospital. No New Year celebration—she again volunteered double shifts over the long holiday.

With the new year, Georgie decided it was time to clean up. Today he shaved and asked Jane, if she had time, would she mind cutting his hair. Draping a towel around his shoulders, Jane snipped off the ponytail with one whack, handing it to Gran, then trimmed the rest.

"Wonderful how a fresh haircut can give a person a lift. At least that's what it does for us women. What's your excuse for spiffing up?" Gran asked.

"I don't know. Just thought it was time."

"Could it be because of a certain person—name begins with an R?" Gran asked.

Georgie answered smiling. "I can't put anything over on you, Gran."

Gran raised her brows, tapping her toe with a bit more vigor.

Jane put away the scissors, shook the towel out the back door. Georgie surprised her by getting out the electric broom, sucking up the bits of hair on the floor. He was a little bent over, but managed anyway.

Setting the kettle on the stove for tea, Jane paused at the window. "Tommy just turned into the driveway. I swear since the incident of the moldy barley, he's here about every day."

"He's a good friend," Georgie said. "We've batted around ideas on who sabotaged the barley and why, as well as ideas about the two men we suspect of stealing the gold bars. Thank God they didn't take all the gold. From what Finn has said, one bar saves the brewpub for another year, maybe more. You Bradleys lucked out big time. I know it's still hard to keep the farm afloat," Georgie said."

"Come on in, Tommy. Georgie's in the kitchen," Jane called out.

"Morning, Jane, Gran. And George, how ya doing big—whoa, look at you. A regular gentleman farmer. Next thing you'll be smoking a pipe and wearing a velvet jacket with leather patches." Tommy laughed, giving Georgie's shoulder a fake punch.

"Cuppa tea, Tommy?" Jane asked.

"Maybe a sip. I stopped by to see if George wanted to go with me to talk to Sam."

"Sounds great. What's on your mind?" Georgie said.

"I'm talking to everyone again who was here the day of the harvest. Sam's farm equipment is where it began when you rented the combine. Thanks, Jane." Tommy shook his head when offered a cube of sugar.

Gran tapped her toe lightly on the floor, keeping her rocker in a slow rhythm as she sipped her tea. All right you two—Tom and George—what's up with the names?"

"Nothing much, Gran," Tommy said. "Just two guys with big boy talk. How's the incision, George?" Tommy asked chuckling.

"Hurt like the devil yesterday, but it's eased off today. I'm in training so I can stash these crutches tomorrow. Get out of Jane and Gran's way."

"I for one have enjoyed your company," Gran said. "And if you don't mind, I'm sticking to Georgie and Tommy."

"Me too," Jane said swapping a high five with Gran.

———

TOMMY PARKED THE BLACK-and-white at the front entrance of the farm equipment rental office. He gave Georgie a hand with the crutches as he got out of the car. Georgie slowly pulled his body to a standing position stopping short of straight up, still a slight bend in his back.

Sam strolled out of the small cement-block building. "Hey, good to see you up and about, Georgie. Come on in. I'm starting to get a few calls for snow blades for pickup trucks. Always a bit slow between Thanksgiving and the first snowfall," Sam said with a sigh. "What brings you by, Tommy, or is our boy here getting cabin fever?"

"Nothing much, just trying to be sure I have the timeline right that day Georgie harvested the barley." Tommy drew out a small tablet from his pants pocket, flicked a few pages. "Sam, you drove the combine and thresher to the farm and Georgie drove it back. Henry came by for a truck. He drove it to the farm but drove it home that night because of the storm. I take it he brought the truck back here in the morning and picked up his car?"

"Yup, that's right, as far as I can remember," Sam said.

"Is Henry around?" Tommy asked.

"No. He's not here much until we get busy with the snowplow guys. We need some snow and I mean more than a dusting. I can't pay him to sit around. From the way he talks these days, I think he hangs out more at Finn's pub. He bought a new car the other day. Likes to show it off."

"Umm, slow here at your shop—a used car?" Tommy asked.

"No, brand new. Rather sporty. A red Mustang. I don't know where he got the money. When I asked, he just laughed. Said I wasn't the only game in town. Must have picked up a mighty big-paying job."

———

TOMMY DROVE BACK TO the farm to drop Georgie off. "Lookie there, George, a red Mustang parked in the handicapped spot at the pub. I'm a bit thirsty for a frosty beer. How about you?"

"My thought exactly," Georgie said. Getting out of the car he almost fell over tucking the crutches into his armpits. "Damn things. When I get to the house, I'm going to try walking without them. Like I said, I'm in training and I'm going to step it up a few notches today."

"Take it easy, my friend. I don't want to put the siren on full blast escorting you back to the hospital."

Tommy slowly walked beside Georgie into the pub. Cameron was talking to Finn behind the bar, a scowl crossing Cam's face when he saw Georgie. "It was stupid to harvest that barley. You've ruined everything, Mr. George Wolfe," Cameron said in a loud spiteful voice.

Finn didn't say anything, but seemed to agree with Cam. No smile on his face seeing Georgie out and about. No words of encouragement.

A few bikers sat at a table hunched over a map discussing routes to Canada.

Henry was sitting at the bar, chuckling. By the look of Finn's face, he didn't think whatever Henry was laughing at was funny.

Tommy moseyed up to the bar, hitching up on a stool. Georgie clip clopped behind Tommy as Finn pulled a chair around.

"What's happening, Henry?" Tommy asked.

"What's happening? Did you see that red sporty number out front?"

"I did," Tommy said, nodding his head when Finn motioned at the tap, offering a beer.

"She's mine. First time I ever had a brand new car. A beauty."

"For sure, a beauty. Must of cost a lot. Big payments I would guess," Tommy said.

"Nah, paid cash. Let's just say it was an inheritance."

"Lucky you, and lucky me finding you here. I was going over my notes, talking to people once more about the harvest, you know when you helped Georgie—the storm."

"You have my statement, Sheriff. So go bug someone else. It's time for me to go to work, fire up Miss Red."

Henry slapped a twenty on the counter. "Thanks for the beer, Finn. Keep the change," Henry said, chuckling as he strolled out into the frigid January air.

Chapter 35

———

SCARPETTI THREW ANOTHER LOG on the fire. The small flame licked the new fuel shooting sparks up the chimney.

"I'm glad you accepted my invitation to share a drink, Cameron. Nice to get to know each other better. I enjoyed our last chat."

"I enjoyed our meeting as well, Mr. Scarpetti. I was moved by your story—your son's horrible death, caught in the horror of the tavern fire. I was going to look up the story on the internet but was sidetracked with the problems I've had at the brewery, my side of the business."

"No need to look up the story. The papers made all kinds of insinuations about my son. Said Logan was known as Scarface, like he was a thug. I'm sorry to hear there are problems at the brewery. Nothing serious I trust?"

"Could have been very serious. We're trying to expand—too fast. Funds are tight. Any hiccup in the business and I'm afraid we'd have to shut it down, maybe worse. You may have heard?" Cameron said.

"No, the town gossips have said nothing. What happened?"

"Georgie—you know him?"

"I've heard of him. A farmer? Lives on Bradley Farm?"

"Yes, he had a bumper crop of barley growing and foolishly harvested it hours before that bad storm.

"Yes, that was quite a storm. But what happened? The barley would have survived."

"Georgie didn't think so. He rented the equipment and began harvesting. Some was caught in the rain, added to the other in the barn. Lost the whole crop—mold set in."

"Are the Bradleys going to have to sell? Surely not. No contingency funds?" Scarpetti said, pouring more amber liquid into their glasses.

"That's what it looked like. But there were gold bricks hidden in the horse barn. Don't ask me how they got there, or how they found them. Some cock-and-bull story about their ancestors. A couple of robbers got wind of the gold."

"Oh, my—rich one day paupers the next. Was all the gold stolen?"

"No, there is one brick they didn't take. Georgie was shot during the skirmish."

"I did hear about that. He survived, I believe?"

"Yes. He's back home from the hospital, a few days ago. Still in rough shape. He's on crutches—staying at the big house."

"Still a piece of gold left—that's good. I'm sure they'll put that in a safe place...haven't they?"

Cameron laughed. "They're crazy. Put the brick in the cellar, behind some shelves of rhubarb, at least that's what Finn said."

"Behind shelves? Surely not?" Scarpetti said, shaking his head.

"Me? I'd have it in a safe deposit box in a Portsmouth bank. But not the Bradleys."

"The Bradleys are losers. You're the brains of the operation, Cameron. I hinted when you were here last, about joining me. I have a thousand acres, looking to buy more. I'm putting together a business plan to sell barley to all the craft beer brewers in New England and over the Canadian border, then expand through the Midwest. I'm looking to brew craft beer for many of the bars, restaurants across the country, be a major distributor. Heck with opening a pub, unless that's something you want to tinker with.

You have to think big my boy. Sorry, I got carried away. You remind me of my son. He had so much promise...taken from me too soon."

Cameron raised his brows. "That's very ambitious. Such an enterprise would have to be well funded."

"The investors are ready. I'm asking you, Cameron, do you want to be the brewmaster of such a large undertaking, create your own label?"

Scarpetti poured another shot of Scotch into Cameron's glass.

Cameron stood, paced to the door leading to the atrium. "That's quite an offer, Mr. Scarpetti."

"Please, call me Vincenzo. What do you say?"

"Give me a little time. I have to think about it."

"I understand. But I've already contracted to clear more of my land. If not you, I do have a brewmaster in Boston who is eager to join me. Two weeks, son. Let me know your answer. Oh, there is one thing I must caution you about. You told me at your last visit that you're married. I have to ask you to keep this offer between us men. You understand, I don't want to alert the Bradleys just yet."

––––––

"FRANKIE, VINCENZO HERE. Did you have a happy New Year celebration—the Boston Pops, fireworks over the Hudson River?"

"Ah yes, Vincenzo. It was spectacular as usual. You. How did you spend the evening?"

"It was quiet, Frankie. Family prefers to winter in Florida, holiday or not. I do have some news, dear friend. Please tell your men the gold is in the cellar of the main house, behind some shelves holding jars of rhubarb."

Giovanni let out a belly laugh. "Rhubarb? Now that's a first. Not to worry. My men will take care of the situation before that rhubarb goes bad. Who knows, maybe they'll drop off a jar for you."

Chapter 36

A WEEK PASSED. An undercurrent of tension in the farmhouse. Gran and Jane felt it, Danny didn't. Whenever Finn, Georgie, and even Wolfe, were in the house at the same time conversation was strained, usually ending with one or the other leaving. Georgie thanked Gran and Jane for the use of a bedroom, but felt it was time to sleep in his own bed.

Georgie stashed the crutches in the corner of his bedroom closet in the tree house. He still couldn't stand up straight, but Rosie told him not to worry when she surprised him a couple of days earlier, visiting the farm with a gallon of chocolate-chip ice-cream for the family. She consoled him, saying it was normal to feel the stitches pulling when he stood—that's all. As soon as he saw the doctor to remove his handy work, he would be good as new. His body would match his new look—short hair, clean shaven—a rugged, very handsome farmer. Her visit was short but long enough to share a brief kiss, both saying how much they missed each other, and both promising to see each other soon.

Finally sleeping in his own bed, Georgie rose in anticipation, in a happy frame of mind. Today he had an appointment to see the surgeon to remove the stitches.

He was careful when walking up the path, careful wherever he walked, not taking a chance of falling, renewing the injury. He smiled. Tommy was driving him to the hospital and he was going to see Rosie. She'd take a quick break—a few minutes was better than no minutes.

Tommy drove up as Georgie emerged from the house after letting Gran know he was leaving for the hospital.

"A beautiful day, my friend," Tommy said.

"That it is. I'm anxious to get on with life, leave my hospital stay behind me, everything that is but Rosie. Tom, I'm in love. I mean really in love."

"Like making plans for the future kind of love?" Tommy asked.

"Not yet. I think we're both enjoying the miracle that we found each other. Every day we're together is a better day. Are you seeing anyone, Tom?"

"Now and then—nothing like you and Rosie."

Both drifted into silent thoughts as the miles sped by.

In short order they arrived at the hospital and Georgie hitched up on the examination table. The doctor checked the incision and then began removing the stitches. Tommy leaned against the wall taking in the process.

"You're a quick healer, George. Without these stitches you're going to feel a whole lot better. I still want you to take it easy for a couple more weeks, and no heavy lifting."

"Okay, doc. When do you think I can get up on the tractor?"

"I'd wait awhile, bedsides the ground's frozen and will be covered in more snow soon according to the weather girl. Has Wolfe said anything to you about your injuries, or anything else that's bothering him?"

"That's a strange question, doc. Dad never lets on that anything's bothering him. Something I should know? Is he sick? Keeping something from me, because I'll ask—"

"Excuse me," the doc said, retrieving his cell phone. Nodding, he stuffed it back in his pocket. "Excuse me. I'll be right back."

Georgie looked at Tommy. Both shrugged.

Georgie eased off the table, pulled up his jeans, pulled his turtleneck sweater down over his head. He walked to the window, turned, glanced around the examination room. He noticed a piece of paper next to the doctor's laptop. His name was at the top in large type. Two paragraphs followed. He picked up the paper and read what appeared to be a report. His hand began to shake as he slumped on a chair.

"What's the matter, George?" Tommy said.

Georgie held out the paper to him as the doctor returned.

"Is it true, doc? What's on that paper? Is that why you asked me if Dad, if Wolfe said anything was bothering him?"

Tommy looked at Georgie, then handed the paper to the doctor.

The doctor looked Georgie in the eyes. "I'm sorry. I didn't want you to find out this way. When the family gave blood to the hospital blood bank in your name, of course, Finn was the star donor with the same blood type, but I found something unique about Wolfe's donation. So unique that I checked what I found, or what I didn't find, with my colleagues as well as experts in the field. They all supported my theory, agreed with my conclusion. You read it. No point in beating around the bush."

"Then it's true, doc?"

"George, the probability of Wolfe being your biological father is zero. When I asked him about it, he admitted as much."

Georgie stared at the doctor, disbelief written across his face, mouth agape. White knuckles gripped the edge of the chair. "That's it? He's not my father? He admitted he wasn't and said nothing more? No explanation? All these years?" Georgie's voice was loud, words clipped.

"I asked if he wanted me to help, be with him when he told you. He said no, that he would talk to you."

"Thanks, doc. We're done? No more visits?"

"No more visits. But remember, you have to ease into your routines on the farm. Operative word—ease. And George, let me know if you want to talk. I know professionals—"

"I'll handle it. But thanks," he said, spitting out the words—*I'll handle it.*

"Let's get out of here, Tom," Georgie said, turning on his heel.

Tommy watched his friend morph from a happy man looking to his future into a man full of anger. His fists were balled, only a slight hump in his shoulders as he charged down the hall, his cell to his ear.

"Rosie, can you meet me in the lobby? Tom and I are heading back to Lakeville. I'm entering the lobby now."

Tommy caught up to him. "Want me to get the car or are you going to talk to Rosie over coffee?"

"Go ahead, get the car. I'll be right out," George whispered, his body wound tight, ready to spring, ready to come out punching. He paced by the elevator waiting for Rosie.

She emerged from the elevator all smiles, ready to kiss Georgie, but stopped short.

"I can't stay, Rose."

Rosie shivered at his using the name Rose, not personal, no warmth.

"What is it, George? Do you have an infection?"

"That dream of yours. What happens when you wake up and it's the same old life you wanted to get away from? What then?"

"I don't know? It's just a dream, a fantasy. What happened?"

"Doc told me that Wolfe's blood held a secret. A secret he kept from me for over forty-six years, seven months, and who knows how minutes. He's not my father."

———

ON THE WAY BACK to the farm, Tommy tried to start a conversation but Georgie wasn't talking. At the base of the driveway, he asked Tommy to drop him off. He thanked him for the ride, then stalked off to the tree house, crutches over his shoulder.

Georgie emerged at dinner time—pot roast, potatoes and carrots—joining the family around the table. The tension between Georgie and Wolfe was palpable, but why? The family shrugged their shoulders, talked quietly about the weather—was it going to snow or not. Anything to breach the silence.

Wolfe helped himself to another spoonful of potatoes, pushed an indentation with his fork, drizzled gravy in the hole. Without looking at Georgie, he pricked the balloon hovering over the table. "What did the doctor have to say, Georgie?"

Georgie's temples were throbbing. "He talked about your blood. Then he revealed quite a shocker. Said that the blood you donated on my behalf clearly showed that you are not my biological father. I was wondering if you could shed some light on the subject of my parentage?"

The family sat in silence, holding their breath, eyes fixed on Wolfe.

Wolfe sighed. "As I told you when we talked down at the lake, your mother and I worked at a bar. But there was more. She became involved with a man who worked with horses, a drifter, one stable to the next. He swept her off her feet. There was this special weekend she spent with him, a romantic weekend it was supposed to be. She was excited and anticipated he would propose. On Monday late afternoon, she showed up for her shift at the bar. She was in tears. He had left her that morning. A couple months later she told me she was pregnant, asked if she could continue to share the studio apartment with me. She was going to keep the baby but didn't want to be alone. The pregnancy proceeded with complications. They were so bad she made me swear that if she died that I wouldn't leave the baby at an orphanage like what happened to her and to me. I was scared.

I told you the rest." Wolfe laid his fork down on the plate next to the untouched potatoes and gravy.

"Not all of it." Georgie's eyes locked on the man sitting across the table from him.

Stunned, Gran looked at Jane, then Danny. Katie asked Daisy to help her clear the table. Finn looked from Wolfe to Georgie.

Georgie stood, turned and slammed out the back door.

He trudged down to the lake, visions of his real father swirling in his head. A bad man. Bad, but he didn't know what he'd done. Still the man could have left his mother with some kind of words, words that he would be in touch. Where is he? Is he still alive?

A horse trainer who moved on after planting his seed. A bad story. A shitty story.

"Hello Betty! Goodbye Betty!"

Chapter 37

———

PEACE ENVELOPED BRADLEY FARM lying under the moon and stars.

A false feeling.

The farm was anything but peaceful.

The lights in the farmhouse were out by nine o'clock. Finn closed the pub and went home to Katie and Daisy in their tiny house by the lake. Finn had no idea where Cam was. He hadn't seen him or Carrie all day.

Wolfe left the dinner table shortly after Georgie. He hesitated at the top of the path, then strode to the tree house, poured himself a stiff drink and went to bed. Georgie's bedroom door was shut. No light slid out from under the door.

The next morning Finn went to the pub to clean up the bar. He saw Cam fiddling with one of the monstrous stainless steel tanks in the brewery.

Daisy ran down the driveway to catch the school bus, Lucas dashing beside her. After she climbed aboard the bus, the dog made a fast retreat to the warmth of the tiny house and treats from Katie, his mistress.

Carrie stepped out of her tiny house, her face drawn from lack of sleep. Lucas was barking for Katie to let him in.

"Hey, Carrie," Katie called out as Lucas squeezed between her legs to his doggie dish. "Can you stay for a cup of coffee?"

"Why not, I need it," Carrie snapped.

Oh, oh, something happened in Fosterville, Katie thought as she poured the remainder of the morning coffee into two mugs. A small carton of cream and the sugar bowl were on the dropdown table.

Katie sat on the narrow bench under a window, leaning back against the throw pillows. She watched her friend take a sip of coffee. A tear meandered down Carrie's cheek, dropping from her chin to the collar of her plaid flannel shirt.

"What happened, Carrie?" Katie's voice was soft. She knew Carrie to be a strong woman, and knew better than to rush to her side. That would come after Carrie shared what was bothering her. The two friends, husbands being business partners and all, had talked when the partnership was signed. They agreed that they would not talk business except to schedule shifts at the pub. They valued their friendship, the only two women on the farm not a Bradley by birth, and certainly didn't want to get caught in the middle of a disagreement—business or whatever.

"Cam hasn't been himself…for a few weeks, a month," Carrie said. "When I asked him why he suddenly developed a burr up his saddle, he scoffed saying that I was imagining things. But then, get this, I could tell there was more to it than the loss of the barley crop. He turned to me and said everything was hunky-dory. He said that the Bradley's luck hadn't run out, that the old man who bought the farm long ago had saved it from foreclosure once again. You know, Katie, you were there that night."

Katie was aware that when Finn's mom and dad were married, his dad went off to war, his grandfather died, and his dad returned home a broken man—in spirit and missing a leg. Gran confided in Jane and Danny's children that it was touch and go for several years when the kids were young. That if it hadn't been for Wolfe, they certainly would have lost the farm.

"Yes, the gold was a lucky find even though Georgie was almost killed when he and Finn interrupted the robbers. But you're right, one gold bar will get the brewpub on firm footing," Katie said.

"Okay, but then what's bothering Cam? If everything is wonderful financially—except for Georgie. Cam says he's a loser," Carrie said, looking to Katie for confirmation.

"A bit harsh, don't you think? Although, in Finn's eyes, some of Georgie's luster has dimmed lately, but—"

"Katie, there's more. Cam's been offered a position, an offer to join another farm as brewmaster. He won't tell me who made the offer, where this other farm is located, or the name of the farm. I asked him, more like yelled at him, how could he expect me to up and move again. I left Colorado where I grew up, left my parents and friends to be with him. We hauled our tiny house, parked a few yards from yours, and now he wants me to come with him to God knows where?" Tears erupted as Carrie's words exploded from her mouth.

Katie knelt in front of her friend, handing her a tissue. "Carrie, do you think Cam is being pressured for an answer? It could explain his moodiness. Or, is the person simply trying to find out if Cam would even consider leaving the brewpub?"

"Oh, it's real all right. He's promised the person that he'd let him know in two weeks."

"Oh my God, Carrie—"

"Katie, you can't tell Finn. I shouldn't have told you, but think if the shoe was on the other foot, and you were up against such a decision—go with your husband or...or leave him. You'd have to talk to somebody wouldn't you?"

Katie felt a spasm up her spine. If Cam left, that would be the end of the brewpub. She took a deep breath, willing herself to stay calm. Sliding a chair beside Carrie, she grasped her hand pulling her into a tight hug. "Yes, I would have to ask for advice, at the very least. I could never hold it in."

Katie stroked Carrie's back, leaned over for another tissue handing it to Carrie to mop her tears.

"Except for the gold, Bradley Farm seems to be under a string of bad luck," Katie said, a sigh crossing her lips.

"What else?" Carrie asked, blowing her nose.

"Last night, Georgie accused Wolfe of holding a terrible secret. Seems when Wolfe gave blood at the hospital not only was it not a match, but that Wolfe couldn't even be his father."

"What? How—" Carrie started to ask.

"Wolfe admitted to the doctor that he wasn't. He had a relationship with a woman he worked with. She became pregnant by some other man, who left her. She died in childbirth and Wolfe assumed the role of the baby's father...something like that. Georgie was that baby."

———

GEORGIE LEFT THE TREE HOUSE, still watching where he stepped. Without crutches, he pulled himself up straight. Taking deep breaths, he headed for the brewpub to check with Cam on the supply of barley he had on hand—did he need more? If the answer was yes, then he had to buy it. Entering through the back door, Cam was standing on the second rung of a ladder attached to a tank. He was reading a gauge, writing down the setting when he looked up.

"Oh, it's you," Cam snapped.

"Just checking, Cam. How many more bags of barely do you need for the month?" Georgie asked, ignoring Cam's sharp tongue.

"I'll tell you when I get around to it. You're such a loser, Georgie. Now get out of my way," Cam jumped down from the ladder, brushed by Georgie to another tank with his notebook.

Georgie smashed through the swinging door to the pub. Finn was adding glasses from the dishwasher to the shelves. "What got into Cameron? I asked him about his barley supply and he bit my head off."

"Well, the mold did happen on your watch," Finn said, turning back to the glasses.

Georgie shook his head. There was nothing more to say.

Chapter 38

GRAN TOE-TAPPED THE floor boards rocking her chair at a fast clip. Her mouth set, eyes staring at the log Danny added to the fireplace. Her morning coffee turned tepid.

"Alright, Mom, you've been rocketing to the moon for more than ten minutes by my count. You've got that look," Danny said.

"What look?" Gran replied with a smirk.

"Scheming—that look. Next, you and Jane will be lighting up one of those cigarillos you girls smoke when you've got something cooking."

Jane chuckled. "I was thinking the same thing, Danny. Come on, Gran. Share!"

Gran shared sending Jane and Danny into a frenzy of activity.

Jane called the hospital, talked to Georgie's surgeon. She talked to Jeli. She marched to Finn's tiny house, gathering a couple of items from Katie, leaving her befuddled.

Danny carefully removed the backing of Bullion's painting, removed the letter, then replaced the backing. Checking the list Gran wrote down for him, he gathered the items, handing them to Gran in her sewing room.

Gran already had a few bits and pieces in her possession, items she had stored in her desk for safekeeping. She added to the cache in a small suitcase, being especially careful that the items remained as pristine as possible. Each one was placed in a plastic bag and carefully labeled—contents identified with date of origin as best as she could determine.

Finished with the tasks Gran laid out, the trio weighed the pros and cons—who would be the best person to bring into their circle, best to track the collection. They unanimously decided on Sheriff Tommy Townsend.

Chapter 39

SOMEONE WAS LEANING ON Scarpetti's doorbell. If there was one thing, among many, that irritated him, it was someone arriving unannounced. He stomped to the front door, yelling as he opened the door. "I don't want—"

"Mr. Scarpetti, we have to talk." Henry pushed his way passed the silver-haired man, then reeled around facing him, hands balled on his hips.

Scarpetti stepped outside. Had anyone seen Henry come into his house? Henry's red car was in the driveway. It could be seen from the road. Scarpetti stepped back inside leaving the front door open.

"What are you doing here, Henry? I told you—"

"Yah, yah, always call first. I came for one thing. When do I get added to the payroll? I showed you I'm a man of action. I took care of that little crop problem of yours and—"

"For which I paid you handsomely."

"Yah, but are you a man of your word? You said you were going to put your acres to work. You said I knew my way around farm equipment. I also know how to clear the land. So, as I see it, if you're a man of your word, I could start clearing the land *now*, which means you have to put me on the payroll *now*."

Henry was a big man, over six feet, bulging muscles. Scarpetti was a little more than five feet. He relaxed his shoulders. "You're right, Henry, as usual. I should have called you. I've been very busy, one thing and another. But you're right, you could start clearing the land, on the payroll, of course. Give me a few days to tidy up my other business."

Scarpetti reached into his pants pocket, pulling out a wad of bills. "Here's two hundred. That should tide you over to next week I would think?"

"But only till next week. A man has to eat and I'm trying to fix up my house."

"Of course, the foreclosure, west side of town. Don't forget I talked to the bank and—"

"Sure, but I'm paying for it. It's a fire trap."

"But now you're a man with property." Scarpetti took a deep breath. "You'd better leave. It wouldn't be good for you to be seen here…not until next week. Come to think of it, maybe I'll put an article in the Portsmouth paper, give what they call a human interest story to the reporter. The story that Anthony Scarpetti is going into farming again. A big operation. And that you, Henry Fogel, will be the foreman. How does that sound?"

"Good, Mr. Scarpetti. Sounds real good."

"Wait for the article my boy. I'll be in touch. Don't let that car of yours run away with you."

"Not a chance. I'll wait for the announcement."

Scarpetti closed the door as soon as the red Mustang turned out of the driveway. He strode to the bar in his office, poured a double shot of whiskey in a crystal highball glass taking a long swallow. Sighing, the whiskey calming his blood pressure, he picked up his phone tapping the first name in the list. The call was picked up on the first ring.

"Vincenzo, my friend, I've been anxiously waiting—"

"Frankie you have to move in the next two days, the last piece of gold. And I have another urgent matter that you can deal with at the same time. In fact, wrap up two loose ends and we'll be in business. The man I sent to you to buy the car, he's become a major liability."

"I see. You worry too much, Vincenzo. My boys will take care of everything. Maybe you should spend the next couple of nights with me, an old friend. We'll go out to dinner, the theatre. A nice evening out. People will see you with me."

"I'll be on my way within the hour, Frankie, my dear, dear friend."

Chapter 40

WINTER HAD SET IN with a vengeance holding Georgie in check, forcing him to ease up, give his body a chance to heal. Standing by his tractor, he opened a can of oil. If he couldn't climb up or put the relic in drive and head out to till the soil, at least he could add oil to her joints. The next time he drove out to the fields she'd purr like a kitten.

The barn door was shut against the blast of frigid wind from the north. He looked up when the door slid open a smidge allowing Tommy to squeeze through, then sliding it shut on its rails.

"Hey, Tom. You're a sight for sore eyes. Finally somebody who won't snarl at me—I hope."

"No, just stopped by to shoot the breeze for a few minutes. I was over at Sam's shop. Those dinosaurs—"

"Harvesting equipment?"

"Yes. Man oh man, when winter comes, that's a bunch of iron sitting idle. Anyway, Henry pulled in the lot just as I was leaving. He didn't want to talk, but I heaved myself in the passenger side of his red toy. I said I had a couple more questions for him. He told me to get out, he'd said all he had to say about your harvest. Clammed up tighter than a can of tuna. He sat fidgeting with the keys dangling from the ignition one minute, turning the engine over the next, only to remove the keys the next. I commented about his new car—nice leather seats, GPS in the console."

"Ha, I bet he loved that."

"Well, that's it. He didn't say anything about his car, just that he was checking out Sam's equipment, told him which ones he liked most to rent come spring. He wanted the best, most powerful. I asked where he was going to use such farm equipment. Bradley Farm? Working for you?"

"What did he say?"

"Said, 'wouldn't you like to know.' Snarly like. Then he told me again to get out of his car, that he was going to be late for an appointment at the seed store."

"He wouldn't buy seed unless someone gave him the money or permission to put it on an account. I sure would like to know where he's getting the dough," Georgie said.

"George, remember when Travis asked if there could be a connection to the moldy barley and the gold robbery? I told you I asked around—came up empty. But, Henry knows something. I feel it in my gut."

"Your gut?"

"Yes, niggles and niggles, causing a knot. Hurts like hell when I can't come up with an answer. You said Henry was in the barn alone for twenty, maybe thirty minutes. Not much time, but..." Tommy pushed his hat up on his forehead. Georgie did the same with his beat up sun hat.

"Yep, something I can't get out of my head, but I can't come up with a connection either," Georgie said.

"Same here. That gold bar still in the cellar at the farmhouse?"

"Sure is. Wolfe rebuilt the shelves. Backed them with a piece of plywood on hinges. It's not very heavy. You can't see the hinges unless you look for them. But if you knew, you can swing the section out easy as pie, then you can see the hole to the underground room."

"You patch things up with Wolfe?"

"Don't ask—don't go there!"

Chapter 41

———

STORM CLOUDS SLID OVER the moon, the stars. The last snow storm had melted away leaving ice patches. Scooter snuggled into his pillow at the foot of Gran's bed. Everyone on the farm had turned in early, exhausted trying to dodge the tension that kept bubbling up out of nowhere. Conversations were cut short or were nonexistent. Wolfe and Georgie weren't talking. Something was bothering Finn and Cameron. They kept sending barbs at Georgie, and Carrie and Katie weren't offering any clues.

Gran was restless. Turning on her side she checked the clock— three minutes past one.

Scooter flipped over on his tummy, ears perking up.

"Not now, Scooter. You have to wait for morning," Gran said, yawning, shifting her pillow.

The little dog jumped off the bed, padding to the hall.

Danny stood on one leg, hand on the bed to steady himself. He saw Scooter wagging his tail in the doorway.

"Jane, you awake?" Danny whispered.

"Yes, I heard it too."

"Call 911. Say it's urgent. Someone's trying to get in the house."

Danny pulled on a slipper, his bathrobe. He opened the nightstand drawer beside the bed, retrieving his revolver. He checked the chamber. It was loaded. He stuffed the gun in his bathrobe pocket. Grabbing his crutches, he swung quietly down the hall to the kitchen, Scooter by his side, hackles raised. Danny paused, head cocked, listening. There it was again a creaky sound.

He shook his head. "Maybe a squirrel, Scooter. Could be a tree limb brushing against the house."

Scooter whined, ears back.

Danny heard the noise again. He slowly stepped to the door at the top of the cellar stairs. The staircase to the cellar was seldom used—steps rickety and in need of repair. It was safer to enter by the bulkhead, the stairs wider, sturdier. He put his ear to the door. Scooter leaned into Danny's crutch.

A light flashed through the kitchen.

Danny stepped to the window. It was Tommy in the black and white. No siren.

Tommy got out of the car, hesitated, drew his gun. Crouching in the bushes, he made his way toward the side of the house out of Danny's sight.

A fire engine streaked passed the farm, wailing in the coal-black night.

Danny opened the cellar door a crack.

He heard muffled footsteps.

The beam of a flashlight swung around the cellar, up the cellar stairs.

Danny slammed the kitchen door, swinging on his crutches to the left of the door.

A bullet pierced the door.

Scooter put his nose in the air—barking, barking.

Another gunshot.

A scream.

Danny swung to the back door. Struggling to open the door, his fingers shaking, he swung outside on his crutches. "Tommy, you OK?" he called out.

"At the bulkhead. Stay where you are. I have someone you'll want to meet."

A shiver ran up Danny's spine. Was Tommy being held at gunpoint? He didn't sound right.

Tommy came around the corner pulling a man in handcuffs. He stopped at the squad car, patted the man down, jerked off the man's backpack, then shoved him in the back seat of the squad car.

"I tell you I didn't do anything wrong. Just looking for a place to get warm. You shot me for nothing. My arm's bleeding," the man hissed bumping his head as he landed in the backseat.

Tommy shut the car door, snatching his cell from his pocket, at its persistent ring.

"What's going on?" Georgie shouted charging up the path, Finn and Wolfe behind him.

Tommy arrested that man in the squad—" Danny started to say.

Tommy yelled at his cell. "What?..."

He stood listening, looking at the ground, up at Danny. "Got it, I'll be there—five minutes." Tommy pocketed the phone, then stuck his hand in the man's backpack drawing out a gold bar. Grinning, he showed it to Danny. "Busy night, Danny. I have to take this to the lab, log it in. Then I'll bring it back to you. Gotta go. There's a house on fire at the edge of town. Finn, can you shut the bulkhead? Button her up? I'll be back in the morning."

"Thanks, Tommy...the bar...everything," Danny called after the Sheriff.

Chapter 42

IT WAS SIX IN THE morning when Danny, fully dressed, opened the back door. He shook Tommy's hand, nodding to him to come in.

There was no chatter around the table. Jane put a fresh pot of coffee to brew. Georgie got up, gave Tommy a hug.

"How are you?" Georgie asked the man who had become his sidekick, his buddy.

"Fine, but it's been quite a morning already. Danny, remember we heard a fire engine when I arrested the guy coming out of your cellar?"

"I do. Where was it going?"

"Seems Henry bought a foreclosure down the road. A man came to his door, barged in, shot him, and left him for dead. The house suddenly exploded in flames. The firemen found Henry crawling out the back door. Before the medics took him to the hospital, I asked him what happened. All he said was that he was held up."

Jane handed Tommy a mug of coffee and set a coffee cake on the table with a knife and stack of small plates.

"Thanks, Jane." Tommy reached down, stroking Scooter's head. "So, now for what else Henry said. First, the fire chief called from the Exeter hospital with an update. That's where I caught up with Henry."

"Wait," Finn said, jumping to his feet. "Who shot Henry and set his house on fire?"

"Deputy Gomer Tipton caught the guy leaving the scene. His hair was singed. He was cussing, stumbling, holding his burned hand. He's in custody. So is the guy I arrested."

"I heard the shot," Danny said.

"Which one? The perp fired his gun before I fired," Tommy said.

"Oh, he put a hole in the cellar door," Danny said pointing to the door.

"That's when I fired—flesh wound. He's bandaged up. Both men are being held in the Portsmouth jail."

"You were saying, about Henry—" Georgie began.

"Henry was terrified. He kept babbling that someone was trying to kill him. He's still at the hospital under sedation for at least the next couple of hours while they treat the gunshot wound, and the burns to his body as he crawled out of the house. I don't know who he was talking about trying to kill him. I don't think it was the intruder—but could have been. The doctor promised to get back to me when I can question him."

"Does he need blood?" Georgie asked.

"He might. The doctor didn't say and I didn't ask. He's lucky to be alive."

"Do you have any leads as to the name of Henry's intruder and the one who attempted to steal the gold bar?" Danny asked.

"All I can say is that I'm working on it. Neither man is talking."

"Something's bothering you, Tom," Georgie said.

"I arrested the perp last night in the cellar. One man. You and Finn interrupted two robbers the night of the first heist. Henry is saying that someone wants him dead. Who? Add the two that Gomer and I arrested during the night—were they working together? A connection? The gold and the moldy harvest like Travis asked."

Tommy shrugged. "Thanks for the coffee and the cake, Jane. I have to get going. I just wanted to bring you folks up to date."

"When will we see you again? When can you give us some answers?" Danny said.

"Maybe tonight. More likely tomorrow."

"Wait, does that include information on the two missing gold bars?" Danny said.

"I don't know," Tommy said over his shoulder as he walked out the back door.

Chapter 43

——

TOMMY AND GOMER SPED SOUTH on I-95 to Boston. What Tommy hadn't revealed to the Bradley family was that the man he arrested in the cellar had a battered business card in his hip pocket. It had a note on the back: *Call when you have it.* The name on the front of the card was Frankie Giovanni known to be a long-time friend of another mob family, the Scarpettis. Vincenzo Scarpetti purchased property in Lakeville, a man who had a running feud with the Bradleys. As of late, he blamed Finn Bradley for the death of Logan Scarpetti, Scarpetti's son.

Tommy thought the animosity between the two Lakeville families had died down. Maybe yes, maybe not. Tommy's gut was screaming at him. He needed answers. Tommy stopped only long enough in Portsmouth to get a search warrant, a search warrant for two gold bars with distinctive markings.

Sheriff Townsend rang the doorbell of the very old brownstone in an upscale Boston neighborhood. A maid answered the door. Townsend flashed his badge as he walked passed her into a large foyer facing a staircase that circled to the second floor. Officers from Boston PD fanned out as Giovanni emerged from a room on the right. The sheriff showed him the search warrant, as two officers mounted the stairs, others entering rooms on the first floor. Their mission was to find the two gold bars and anything else relating to the robbery.

Scarpetti saw the sheriff through a crack in the door that Giovanni had left open. Scarpetti picked up the gold bars on Giovanni's desk, then made a hasty exit to the kitchen and out the back door to the street. Taking long strides, he crossed the street and turned the corner to the T-stop. Smiling to himself, he climbed aboard, rode out to Alewife Station, where he parked his car. He was back in Lakeville in less than two hours since leaving Boston. Home again, he poured himself a stiff drink while contemplating his next move. He checked the telephone directory on his desk, punched the number he wanted on his cell. When the phone was picked up, he identified himself.

"Hello, Mr. George Wolfe, I believe?"

"Yes, but why are you calling?" Georgie said, glancing at the caller ID.

Scarpetti ignored the question. "Vincenzo Scarpetti here. I wonder if I might have a word with you?"

Georgie sucked in some air letting it out slowly. "What about, Mr. Scarpetti? I really don't—"

"Business, my dear man. Just a little business proposition. Now would be a good time. I think you might be interested in my proposal."

"Hmm, but I can't stay long."

———

TOMMY AND THE OTHER officers left Giovanni's mansion empty handed—no gold bars were found. He and Gomer drove back to the Exeter hospital to check on Henry. Badly burned, suffering a lot of pain, he was in no mood to take the rap for Scarpetti. The man had not visited him in the hospital and that spoke volumes to Henry. He was just another pawn in Scarpetti's game to bring down the Bradleys.

Tommy was in no mood to be messed with either. If Henry wanted to play hardball, he was ready.

"Come on, Henry, the moldy barley has your fingerprints all over it, to say nothing about the gold bars. The mob is going to hang you out to dry. A bit player." Tommy hit him hard on all fronts that seemed connected, hoping the man would crack and admit to something.

"It wasn't my idea, you know. Scarpetti...he threatened me. Oh, at first he said I was going to work for him, on the payroll. No, that wasn't first. First he offered me a large sum of money for..."

"For what Henry?" Townsend loomed over the hospital bed, his eyes boring into the man quivering now and then from the pain spasms racking his body. "I'm asking nicely, Henry. Maybe you'd like to be thrown in a cell in Boston. Their interrogation may not be so kind. I ask you again, he gave you a large sum of money for what?"

"All I had to do was water the grain down when I got the chance. The storm...it was perfect. Scarpetti gave me a canister, a nozzle like that screwed on the hose in the horse barn. I did a good job. Scarpetti said I did a good job. Told me to see his friend in Boston, he had a car—new, great price, just for me."

"Do you know what was in the canister, Henry?"

"No. He just said to put it on the end of the hose. Scarpetti is who you want. He threatened me."

"Threatened? Gave you money to buy your car, that's not a threat, more like you were working for him."

"No, it wasn't like that. It wasn't what he said but how he looked me. I felt if I didn't do what he said, he'd see I didn't work around here again, but if I did he'd reward me. Oh, yah, he paid me, but then he turned on me. It was one of his goons that set my house on fire. Scarpetti's got it in for the Bradleys you know."

Tommy heard enough. He left the hospital and drove straight to Scarpetti's. Pulling into the driveway he was surprised to see Georgie's truck. Striding to the front door, Tommy rang the bell.

Yelling penetrated the door. If he wasn't mistaken it was Georgie yelling at Scarpetti and Scarpetti yelling back. Tommy tried the door. It wasn't locked. He opened it in one swift action.

Scarpetti was startled to see the sheriff in the doorway. He drew his gun, reeled Georgie in front of him.

"Get out of my house, Sheriff, or you can say goodbye to your pal here. We were just having a little discussion."

"Calm down, Scarpetti. I'm here to ask a few questions that's all. You see Henry, your employee Henry Fogel, had some nasty words to say about your little arrangement with him."

"That snake is lying."

Tommy caught sight of Danny sneaking out of the kitchen to the foyer. He was pointing a revolver at Scarpetti's back.

"I think not Vincenzo," Danny yelled. "Drop the gun, or I swear I'll end our little feud right here, right now."

Scarpetti whirled around. Georgie dove to the floor. Tommy pounced, stripping the gun from Scarpetti's hand. He fell to the floor screaming in pain that his wrist was broken, at the same time scrambling on the floor for his gun.

Tommy kicked the gun away and cuffed Scarpetti. Pulling his cell from his belt, he called Gomer to make fast tracks to Scarpetti's house.

Disconnecting the call, he looked up at Georgie. "You okay?"

"Yep, I was never so glad to see you. Why—"

"Henry. He sang like a canary. He was the one who sprayed water on your barley. What he didn't know—the canister was full of DDT. The water he sprayed on the grain was laced with it."

Chapter 44

———

FEBRUARY FIRST AND EVERYONE on Bradley Farm was breathing a sigh of relief. Tension remained between Wolfe and Georgie. Georgie left the room if Wolfe entered, or he turned away if Wolfe was there first. The only time they were seen together was at dinner time and then they changed their usual seats at the table—opposite sides, opposite ends.

Cameron confessed to Finn that he had been approached by Scarpetti to join a consortium of craft breweries he was establishing. Confessed that he had been very flattered and had considered it. Flattered to be sought out by the wealthy man but realized Scarpetti was all talk just trying to get back at Finn, blaming him for his son's death. Cameron divulged that he had approached the sheriff's deputy for information about the feud between the Bradleys and the Scarpettis. Gomer was more than willing to tell him the real story about the brewpub.

Cameron, a proud man, didn't beg Finn to overlook the past few months. Scarpetti had approached him, not the other way around. He still wanted to be a partner in the brewpub.

Finn talked to Katie. "I'm not one to hold a grudge," he said.

"Truth is, Finn, you need Cam as much as he needs you. I say keep the partnership, but in the future, if he has doubts about the business he should talk to you about his concerns. Both of you should let bygones be bygones," Katie said. "And I think you should talk to Pops and your mom. Get their opinion. After all, they have a major stake in the future of the brewpub."

Finn kissed his wife, held her close. "I love you, Katie Bradley."

"Love you back. I gave you my thoughts, now go talk to your parents."

TOMMY DROVE UP TO the farmhouse. It was dinner time but he had just come back to Lakeville from Portsmouth. It looked like he and Portsmouth PD could close the Bradley Farm case except for the trials. He smiled as he climbed out of the car—dinnertime at Bradley Farm. He had a hankering for a good home-cooked meal.

As usual, Jane was at the sink and saw the sheriff's car come up the driveway. Danny opened the back door.

"Just in time, Tommy. Jane's fixed enough chicken fried steak for an army. I hope you'll stay for dinner. We're all here. Do you have an update?" Danny said.

"Yes, I'll tell you my story and I'd love to stay for some of that chicken fried steak. And mashed potatoes, I hope?"

Georgie poured the wine as everyone took their seats around the table.

Danny said grace, and then everyone lifted their wine glasses to Tommy, toasting him in thanks for his diligence. With the first sip of wine, their eyes were on him. They were ready and eager for more information.

Tommy tasted his wine and then set the glass down. "Scarpetti is being held on felony charges—breaking and entering, and the theft of the gold bars. While he didn't do the actual theft, he was the mastermind and was in possession of the gold bars at the time of his arrest," Tommy said. He took another sip of his wine, stood, paced to the window then continued.

"No matter how much Scarpetti whined that he didn't do anything wrong, laying the blame on Frankie Giovanni, that it was all Giovanni's idea, the proof came down on Scarpetti's head. The two goons Gomer and I arrested the night of the fire swore they worked for Scarpetti. Henry Fogel is in the Portsmouth jail awaiting trial. He faces jail time for destruction of property with the potential of causing death through grain laced with DDT if the beer had found its way to market. The whole nasty business will be chronicled in the Portsmouth Herald this weekend."

Georgie watched Tommy. Something was wrong. His friend had the niggles again.

Jane, Jeli, Katie and Daisy sprang into action. "Tommy, for goodness sake, sit down and try some of this home cooked food," Jane said.

"Believe I will," Tommy said. "Looks mighty good."

Chapter 45

———

Valentine's Day

A JAM SESSION IN THE pub was in high gear, rocking out the music. Sadie, Jeli, and Finn were perched on high stools strumming their guitars, singing to the applause of the townies.

Red and white streamers, strung with red and white hearts and decorated with silver and red glitter, twirled in the rising tempo of the music—couples dancing and singing along with the trio. Not only was it Valentine's day, not only was it Rosie's birthday, but the end of winter was in sight.

Daisy was dressed in a new frock, white with red roses and hearts appliquéd on the skirt. Red bows were tied on the ends of her pigtails, her feet clad in Mary Jane shoes. White knee-high stockings completed her Valentine outfit.

With spring around the corner, the Bradleys were celebrating plans for expansion. With the gold came relief from fretting season to season, terrified they weren't going to make it to the next season, all thanks to the first Marshall Bradley. Gran's steady hand kept the plans grounded--*expand, but don't be frivolous. Money doesn't last forever, you know.*

Sadie had been working on her first draft of *Rosemary's Story.* A story of a runaway slave who found love on the Underground Railroad, gave life to a baby boy, only to die in childbirth. A story telling how her lover kept her close to him burying her body in the cellar. The story richer with Marshall's letter, his love for Rosemary, and leaving a fortune hidden in a horse barn.

Tommy along with Gomer sat at a table toward the back. The men always on duty, trained to keep an eye out for any wrong doers. Tommy whispered to Gomer that he wanted the family to meet in the back of the pub, in the brewery, as soon as the guitar trio finished the current rendition of Moon River. Gomer nodded and began spreading the word to the family.

Gran ambled toward the brewery, Jane and Danny on either side. Wolfe a few steps behind, nodded to Tommy as he pushed through the swinging doors from the bar into the brewery. The gleaming stainless steel tanks, more than nine feet high, dwarfed everyone. Finn kissed Katie on the cheek, then took Daisy's hand as the little family strolled with Jeli, Sadie, and Travis into the brewery.

Marshall and Anna had joined the family. When Sadie called him in Tel Aviv, that there was going to be a big celebration on Valentine's Day, he quickly planned a business trip to Boston so he and Anna could be with the family. It was also whispered that maybe Georgie had finally met someone, and Valentine's Day was that someone's birthday.

Tommy entered the brewery leaving Gomer at the door to see nobody intruded on the family gathering.

Gran, Jane and Danny could hardly breathe with excitement. Why was Tommy bringing them together—was it good news, or bad news?

Tommy stepped on the first rung of the ladder on the nearest tank overlooking the assembled group before him.

"He looks serious, Danny," Jane said.

"I hope he's not going to spoil the party," Gran said, her excitement deflating.

"Hey, everyone. Excuse the drama but I do have something important to tell you. It has to do with the gold robbery."

"No, no," Finn spoke up. "You're not going to ruin our celebration are you?" he asked with a chuckle.

"That's for you to decide after I finish. Anyway, when George was shot and needed blood, it was discovered that he had a rare type. It also came to light that Finn, here, had the same type. It's my recommendation that the two of you should travel through the rest of your lives within a one-mile radius." Tommy laughed as Finn looked over and grinned at Georgie.

It seemed the two old friends had come to an understanding. All the issues bothering them was dealt with. They all knew that during the ordeal of the past few months, Finn blamed Georgie for negligence during the harvest and the ensuing prospect that the brewpub might have to be closed. But then Georgie was proved correct in his believing it was sabotage.

"The reason I've asked you to meet with me, is that I received a final report today from the Portsmouth PD lab. A report with their results of the investigation I asked them to do. Included in their report were the opinions and analysis of three doctors from the Portsmouth hospital. All involved in producing the report came, one by one, to a unanimous opinion. Let me add that what I sent to the lab were items gathered by Gran, Danny and Jane," Tommy said.

"Tommy, for heaven's sake, you're driving us crazy. Just come out with it," Sadie said. "Do we all have some rare disease? Are you telling us to write our wills?"

"No, Sadie, that's not it. No rare disease. But, piecing the DNA together, the DNA of the items, a story was revealed. Let me back up a step to the blood type issue. There are blood types with subtypes, many subtypes. Some subtypes can raise havoc. Some carry antigens which can trigger an immune response if they are foreign to the body. Also, some AB negative blood can show a higher amount of one ethnic group, say African American."

"Are you saying my blood contained such a subtype?" Finn asked.

"Not yours, Finn. George's. When accepting blood for a transfusion, such as yours, Finn, the closer the match the better chance there was of George's body accepting the blood. As we can all see, George's body accepted your blood, Finn, and he had a speedy recovery…thanks to you."

Tommy took a big gulp of air. Gran's eyes were riveted on him. "So… the lab and the doctors examined what I already mentioned—a box of items from the Bradley clan back to and including the first Marshall Bradley who bought the farm and built the farmhouse. One such item was the lock of his hair in an envelope in the back of Rosemary's journal. The lab took samples of DNA from each item—Jeli gave Gran Rosemary's hairbrush. I believe you all know from the journal Georgie and Finn found, who Rosemary was. Our small lab in Lakeville still had a bone from the skeleton found in the cellar that Danny's dog dug up years ago. You can all ask Gran, Jane and Danny about what they gathered from each of you."

With raised brows, eyes glanced from one to the other, all except Gran. She was grinning at Tommy and he was grinning back at her. Gran's instincts had been spot on.

"What are you trying to say, Tommy? Out with it." Jeli said giggling, her red curls sparking in anticipation.

"Wait, there's more," Tommy said. "The DNA combined with everything else, means with a high, *a very high* probability, that George is a Bradley. And …" Tommy paused. "And…George's AB negative shows a blood subtype of African American—while the probability isn't as high, dare I say carried down from Rosemary?"

Tommy grinned from ear to ear. The Bradley clan was taking in the high probability that Georgie was one of them. Just like they had always felt in their hearts.

Danny hugged Gran, then Jane. "Gran, you were right."

Everyone else, standing in the forest of brew tanks, was in shock as they chattered in whispers. Georgie leaned against the wall, hands locked on top of his head, disbelief on his face. Finn was the first to pull Georgie into an embrace.

"I guess you won't mind my calling you bro? Right, bro?" Finn said.

Tears were cascading down Georgie's cheeks.

Marshall pulled a handkerchief from his pants pocket, handing it to Georgie. "Welcome to the family, Georgie," Marshall said.

Jeli was next, on tip toe, giving Georgie a peck on each cheek. "Welcome to the family,"

Sadie moved in. "Georgie, it's an honor to call you my brother. I suggest you take Rosie outside, get some fresh air and then we'll sing happy birthday to both of you. How about that?" Sadie said. "I love you."

Georgie nodded then looked for Rosie. She was standing by the door. Jeli was giving her a hug. Whatever she said brought a smile to Rosie's lips.

Georgie stepped to Gran. "We have to talk," he said.

"I agree, but not tonight. There's plenty of time."

"Plenty," Jane said squeezing his arm.

From the other side, Danny put his arm around Georgie's shoulders. "If only our ancestors could talk. What a tale that would be."

"I guess they did talk, Danny. And you, Jane and Gran put the words together. Now, if you'll excuse me, I want to check on Rosie."

———

GEORGIE AND ROSIE STEPPED out of the pub into a star-filled night. He took off his jacket wrapping it around her shoulders then pulled her into his arms.

"Quite a night, Rosie."

"Did you ever think—"

"Never. I want you to know the probability that I love you is one-hundred percent. Tell me you love me."

"George, I loved you from the moment you sat down with your coffee at the coffee house."

Georgie kissed her forehead, each cheek, then pressed her to him. "Me too, but I didn't realize it at the moment. Are you still okay with our plan?"

"Yes, I am. You?"

"Absolutely. Let's go inside. Sadie says they want to sing happy birthday to you."

"I heard her and to you, your birth into the Bradley family."

When Georgie and Rosie stepped in the door and embraced, the crowd whooped and hollered. Then Sadie, Finn, and Jeli hitched up on the stools and broke into a fast, happy birthday chorus. Everyone in the pub joined in along with the Bradleys.

His arm around Rosie's waist, Georgie walked up to Danny, Gran, and Jane seated with Wolfe.

"Gran, I want your permission. I've asked Rosie to move into the tree house with me. If she still wants me by the end of the year, Christmas time, I've asked her to marry me."

"You don't need my permission. Of course, we all agree that Rosie is more than welcome to join our crazy family. Right, Danny? Jane?" Gran said.

"Absolutely, Rosie dear," Jane said, giving Rosie a hug.

"Wolfe, I like Georgie's plan," Gran said. "How about you move into the farmhouse? Plenty of bedrooms. We old fogies can play checkers."

"Sounds good to me, Gran. Young lovers don't need an old fogie, as you say, hanging around."

Georgie looked at Wolfe.

Wolfe stared him in the eyes, neither moving a muscle.

Gran whispered, "Georgie, you're lucky Wolfe stepped up to be a father figure when your mother died. Not many men would have done what he did."

Georgie closed the distance to Wolfe, opened his arms, and hugged him tight. "Forgive me. I was struggling, felt lost, disconnected, questioning who I am. Now I'm part of a loving family. If it wasn't for you carrying me up the Bradley's driveway, my question would never have been answered. You didn't abandon me. Thank you. I love you...Dad."

"I love you too, son," Wolfe whispered, drawing Georgie into a fierce hug.

"I guess you could say the Bradleys have come full circle," Gran said, dabbing her eyes. "A baby left in a church over a hundred years ago, and a baby in a basket is brought to our door by a special messenger."

"Serendipity, Gran?" Wolfe whispered.

"I think so. You were destined to be that messenger."

———

GRAN LOOKED AT JANE. Jane nodded. Both grinning, they looked at Danny. He nodded back—their Adirondack chairs were positioned out on the deck. He walked ahead of them, held the door as they sauntered out picking up their jackets from the peg on the way. It was time for a recap of the day.

Bundled up from the cool February night, Jane retrieved the pack of cigarillos from her pocket, offering one to Gran. Pulling a lighter from her other pocket, she leaned over, lit Gran's and then her own. Both women settled back, releasing the first puff, the smoke dissolving in the air.

"Quite a day, Janie," Gran said. Scooter jumped up on her lap, settling with his nose between his paws as she patted his head.

"I like Rosie," Jane said.

"I really like her," Gran said. "Did you catch how they look at each?"

"I remember looking at Danny that way...still do at times," Jane said.

"Marshall and Anna seem happy."

"Yes, they do," Jane said.

"Do you think they'll ever move to Boston...leave Tel Aviv?"

"I don't know." Jane leaned her head back as she reached over patting Gran's hand.

"That Daisy is a hoot. I wouldn't mind seeing another baby or two," Gran said with a chuckle. "After all you had twins."

"Maybe Sadie and Travis," Jane said. "Jeli, flitting around the world. Hope she finds someone, but right now she seems happy with her life."

"So many generations..." Gran said.

"Georgie a Bradley. What did Tommy say the probability was?"

"Change probability to possibility...anything is possible," Gran said.

"All the trials and tribulations we've gone through the past few years..." Jane's words trailed off as she gazed at the stars.

"All in all we have an incredibly loving family," Gran said, reaching for Jane's hand, giving it a squeeze. "We're lucky, Janie."

Epilogue

FRANKIE GIOVANNI SAVORED HIS DRINK, waiting for his wife to join him. He was taking her out to dinner and the theater. He chuckled as he struck a match, touched it to the tip of his Cuban cigar. Taking a puff, he raised his glass. "To you my dear Vincenzo Scarpetti, wherever you are. So sorry our little arrangement didn't work out. But I have every intention of carrying out your plan. I've put together investors, put an offer on your land. You see I'm going into the business of brewing craft beer. I know how much you detest the Bradleys."

He grinned at his reflection in the mirror over the fireplace. It was never revealed to Sheriff Townsend that Giovanni had a close family friend who arranged for the two goons who perpetrated the original theft, and the same goons a little while later splitting the final assignment. One lifting the third gold bar, the other taking care of Henry and setting the fire. Giovanni told them that if they were caught they were to swear Scarpetti hired them. If they swore to this story, they would be paid handsomely after doing their jail time.

Giovanni refreshed his drink. "Ah, yes, my dear friend. I look forward to bringing your dream to a handsome business. Maybe I'll visit you some day, share what I've been able to build. But alas, I fear you may not be pleased."

The End

REVIEW REQUEST

Please consider leaving a review for the eBook edition of my book. The reason I'm asking for reviews: reader reviews are the lifeblood of an author's career. For a long-ago typewriter-jockey like myself, getting reviews (especially on Amazon) means a lot to me and your fellow readers.

It's easy. Log into Amazon, search for the book **TAP** Customer Reviews at the top of the page. **Click**: Write a Customer Review.

Thank you!

ADD ME TO YOUR MAILING LIST

Please shoot me an email to be added to the list for future book launches:

MaryJane@MaryJaneForbes.com

Website: MaryJaneForbes.com

Bradley Family Tree

Marshall Bradley
1810-1880
|
Kenneth Bradley
1845-1920
|
Mason Bradley
1896-1946
|
Arnold Bradley
1927-1970
|
Daniel Bradley
1951 -

Offspring
Jane and Danny Bradley

Twins
Sadie & Marshall
|
Finn
|
Jeli

Wolfe's son
Georgie

Acknowledgements

With the last book in the Bradley Farm series, it was important to me to wrap up loose ends, especially from book one—the beginning of Rosemary's story. Thanks to the following for accompanying me on the journey:

Molly Tredwell—thanks for your constant support and big picture perspective, adding depth, as well as dragging emotions out of the Bradley Farm clan. And then there's your magic with descriptions.

Peggy Keeney—thanks for hanging in there with me. Your ability to catch errors in the timeline, and everything else are invaluable.

Roger and Pat Grady—for your suggestions and honest assessments. I appreciate your time spent on my projects.

Geri Rogers—thanks for your help as always. You may have moved back to your beloved Cape Cod, but our friendship is strong no matter the miles.

Lois Gerber—thanks for the cups of tea, medical tips, and the final review.

Pamela Leone—thanks for sharing your mother's priceless sayings.

Cover design: by Angie: pro_ebookcovers

———

Ancestry DNA: "Send for the kit and let the discoveries begin."

The Underground Railroad, Raymond Bial, Houghton Mifflin Company, New York, NY, 1995

Georgie

ISBN: 978-0-9847948-8-1 (sc)
Printed in the United States of America
Todd Book Publications: 4/2017
Port Orange, Florida

Author photo: Geri Rogers

Author's Note

Bradley Farm Series

After three years, I'm saying goodbye to Bradley Farm. It's with a sense of nostalgia that I leave New England. But, I guess there comes a time when one must move on. Other locations are clamoring for my attention.

———

cozy, romantic mysteries
with a thriller now and then
all filled with suspense

———

Website: MaryJaneForbes.com

READ NEXT?

The Mailbox

Elizabeth Stitchway, Private Eye, Series, Book 1

She delivers mail by day and solves mysteries by night. But when a hurricane reveals a dead body, will her first case be her last?

Elizabeth "Stitch" Stitchway dreams of becoming a private investigator, but she remains stuck in her mail carrier day job. When a freak hurricane tosses her and her truck into fast-moving waters, a mysterious stranger is her only saving grace. But after a dead body bubbles to the surface, her raw PI instincts aren't sure if her savior is a witness or a suspect...

When Stitch starts to receive letters from her protector, she dives head first into a murder investigation. As she searches for clues, the mystery man asks her for help at the expense of her postal responsibilities. But will trusting the suspect make her the next victim?

The Mailbox is a PI murder mystery filled with clever twists and turns. If you like smart female investigators, puzzling plots, and page-turning surprises, then you'll love Mary Jane Forbes' parcel of thrills.

Buy *The Mailbox* to unwrap a package of suspense today!

THE MAILBOX

Priority: Murder

Books by Mary Jane Forbes

DroneKing Trilogy
A Toy Drone for Christmas

Bradley Farm Series
Bradley Farm, Sadie, Finn
Jeli, Marshall, Georgie

The Baker Girl
One Summer, Promises

Twists of Fate Series
The Fisherman, a love story
The Witness, living a lie
Twists of Fate, daring to dream

Murder by Design, Series:
Murder by Design
Labeled in Seattle
Choices, And the Courage to Risk

Elizabeth Stitchway, PI, Series
The Mailbox, Black Magic,
The Painter, Twister

House of Beads Mystery Series
Murder in the House of Beads
Intercept, Checkmate
Identity Theft

Novels - standalone
The Baby Quilt ... a mystery!
The Message...Call Me!

Short Stories

Once Upon a Christmas Eve, a Romantic Fairy Tale
The Christmas Angel and the Magic Holiday Tree

Visit: www.MaryJaneForbes.com